"If you don't give me what I came for then we'll kill your sister."

Aggie surreptitiously wrapped her fingers around the handle of a cast-iron skillet. "And you'll kill her even if I do."

"What makes you think we haven't already?" He took another step toward her, his lips curled into a snarl. "What a waste finding out she wasn't you," he said, unaware of her newfound weapon. The darkness kept her slight movements hidden.

The front door jerked several times. Bronson peered in through the window again. "Aggie? Are you okay?"

She didn't answer and returned her focus back on the large man walking toward her. One more step and he'd be within reach. She raised her gaze to his and lifted her chin. "I've already scared off your little friends parked in my driveway and there's no way I'm giving you anything."

He smirked. "We'll see about that."

With a quick lunge, he came at her full force.

Shannon Redmon remembers the first book she checked out from the neighborhood bookmobile, sparking her love of stories. She hopes to immerse readers into a world of faith, hope and love, all from the beautiful scenery of her North Carolina mountain home, where she lives with her amazing husband, two boys and white foo-foo dog named Sophie. Connect with Shannon on Twitter, @shannon_redmon, or visit her online at www.shannonredmon.com.

Books by Shannon Redmon

Love Inspired Suspense

Cave of Secrets
Secrets Left Behind
Mistaken Mountain Abduction

Visit the Author Profile page at LoveInspired.com.

MISTAKEN MOUNTAIN ABDUCTION

SHANNON REDMON

LOVE INSPIRED SUSPENSE

INSPIRATIONAL ROMANCE

LOVE INSPIRED® SUSPENSE
INSPIRATIONAL ROMANCE

ISBN-13: 978-1-335-58838-8

Recycling programs
for this product may
not exist in your area.

Mistaken Mountain Abduction

Love Inspired
22 Adelaide St. West, 41st Floor
Toronto, Ontario M5H 4E3, Canada
www.LoveInspired.com

Printed in U.S.A.

And ye shall know the truth,
and the truth shall make you free.
—*John* 8:32

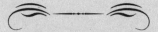

To my sweet boys, Chase and Bryson.
God gave us the best gift when He gave us you.
I pray you will always seek God's truth
and live His words with love for all of your days.

ONE

A child's screams pierced the cold March wind and rushed against former Army Lieutenant Aggie Newton as she exited Sal's Diner. Holly, her six-year-old niece, sat fastened in the back seat of her twin sister's red sedan, alone. Her mother, Leslie, was nowhere in sight.

Aggie bolted across the strip mall parking lot. All her military instincts heightened, as she wove through layers of cars, hoping for any sign of her sister. Leslie would never leave her young daughter alone without supervision, especially in the car.

Not willingly, anyway. She was paranoid about someone snatching her little girl after she filed a restraining order against her abusive ex-husband. He'd threatened to kidnap their daughter and Leslie barely let Holly out of her sight.

Tires screeched to Aggie's right. A white van skidded onto the road, barely missing another vehicle which darted into the grass to prevent a collision. They sped away before Aggie could catch sight of the tag, much less the driver.

More screams permeated the air. Aggie willed her legs to move faster but time waned and quickened simultaneously. Holly was only fifty feet away, but the distance felt like a mile. She had to get to her.

Adrenaline pumped Aggie's heartbeat into her ears and her breaths shortened into bursts. She took note of other bystanders nearby, drawn in by the commotion. A fierce protectiveness rose within Aggie, and she placed her hand on her weapon in case she needed to protect her niece.

"They took Mommy! Aunt Aggie, they took Mommy!" Her niece tugged at the seat belt, trying to get the buckle unfastened.

Lipstick, an open container of mints, and a pen from her sister's purse had fallen to the pavement. Holly held up her arms when Aggie reached her, the young girl's face blotched with tears. She kissed her niece's forehead, unbuckled the strap across the booster seat, then pulled her into her arms. "It's okay. I'm here. You're safe."

A couple approached them—an older man and woman. "Are you all okay?" the man asked.

"Who took your mommy, sweetie?" The

woman stepped closer, but Holly ducked her head against Aggie's shoulder and didn't respond. Aggie held up her hand to keep the woman back. She didn't trust anyone at the moment.

"We'll be okay. Thank you for checking on us. I'm going to call 911," Aggie said, pulling her phone from her pocket and dialing the emergency number. The man nodded, placed an arm around his wife's shoulders and escorted her away.

Her niece's sobs quieted to soft whimpers after a few moments. Aggie continued to stroke the little girl's curls and waited for the operator to answer.

"911. What's your emergency?"

"I'm at Sal's Diner on Main Street in Mills Creek. My sister was just abducted. I think she's in a white van, headed west on highway twenty-five. I'm in a red sedan still in the parking lot."

"What's your name, ma'am?"

"Aggie Newton."

"Are you alone?"

"My six-year-old niece is with me."

"I'm sending officers and an ambulance to your location. Stay where you are until they arrive. Are you hurt?"

"No. Just shaken up a bit."

"Units are on their way."

Aggie put the phone on mute and whispered in Holly's ear, "Can you tell me what happened?"

"Mommy buckled me in. But before she could get into the car, two men pulled her into a van."

The little girl started crying again. Aggie squeezed her tighter and hated to press but details were most vivid after a trauma and if she was going to understand a clear picture of the situation, she needed Holly to talk. "Do you remember what they looked like?"

"They had hoods on, but one man had black, bushy eyebrows and mean eyes."

"Anything else?"

"I don't remember."

"What about the van? Was it white?"

Her niece shrugged her shoulders. "I think so."

"Did you see the license plate?"

She shook her head. "I want Mommy." The sobs returned.

"I know, sweetie. We're gonna find her. Don't you worry. The more you can tell me, the more it will help, okay?"

Aggie searched through her phone's contacts and pulled up a number she hadn't touched in a year. Detective Bronson Young was one of

Mills Creek's most decorated officers, closing more cases with his partner than any other team. If anyone could find her sister, Bronson could, if he'd take her call. He'd always been a kind man who she could count on no matter their past circumstances.

She tapped his number.

"Aggie?"

His deep voice stirred up feelings she'd buried, after they ended their years-long relationship over continued absences, multiple deployments, and military secrets she couldn't discuss.

"Someone took Leslie. I'm at Sal's on Main. Can you come?"

"What do you mean?"

"Two men abducted her. She's been kidnapped."

"On my way. Are you alone?" Chair wheels scraped across the floor and filtered through the phone speaker.

"Holly's with me, but we're fine."

"I'm not far from Main Street. Should be there in five."

Bronson's dependability was one of the many things she missed. They'd dated for years while she served in the United States Army as a Black Hawk helicopter pilot. After they split, he returned home without her. Letting him go was one of the hardest things she'd ever done and never wanted to do again. But this was her sister and Leslie's life was more important than Aggie's awkward feelings.

She hugged her niece tighter as distant sirens echoed through the air. The cashier, who checked her out earlier, pushed her way through the growing crowd and walked over to the vehicle. She pointed a blue glittered nail at Holly. "Is she okay?"

"She will be. Did you see anyone near my sister when I was paying? Our car was in your line of sight behind me."

"I saw a white van pull in and stop in front of the car. I thought he was waiting on a space to open up. That happens a lot."

"Did you get a look at anyone's face?"

Her gaze dropped to Holly. "No. I'm so sorry. I only looked for a couple of seconds and then that handsome man distracted me with his tip."

Palmer Sterling, the CEO of Sterling Securities, had talked to Aggie about working for his company while she was paying the bill. He'd captivated the cashier's attention.

"By the time I looked back, the van was gone. I figured he found another space." The cashier looked back at the diner then faced Aggie again. "Why don't y'all come inside? I'll get you some hot tea or coffee…on the house. Sal won't mind."

Another frigid wind blew across them. Aggie stood, noting Holly's tightened grip and the way her niece shivered against her. The trauma and outside temperature were too much for a six-year-old.

Aggie stepped from the vehicle, her legs heavy as she held Holly and maneuvered from the car. Rapid puffs of fog exhaled with her shallow breaths. She fought back tears welling in her eyes and mouthed a silent prayer of protection for her sister.

The cashier, who was several steps ahead of her, glanced back. "You coming?"

Aggie nodded and trudged up the small hill to the last place she'd seen her sister before she disappeared.

Detective Bronson Young sped through the streets with his blue lights and sirens activated. He hadn't heard from Aggie Newton since he'd ended their relationship a year ago. He often regretted the decision, but after his brother was killed in combat, he didn't want to live every day wondering if the woman he loved would be killed in action. Nor was he the kind of man to ask her to give up her military career. She was one of few women who achieved the difficult task of becoming a Black Hawk helicopter pilot and even though he admired her achievements, the job was the main reason for their breakup.

His phone rang, interrupting his trip down memory lane and he tapped the screen to answer his partner's call. "Young here."

"I got the information on Corbin's death from the Freedom of Information Act form you filed. Most of the contents are redacted and doesn't give us anything new."

Detective Oz Kelly had been helping him on the side with his brother's case. Something Aggie was forbidden to do. He understood military information was often classified, and in some ways, admired her loyalty to keep those secrets. But he needed answers and being shut out of so much when it came to his brother, was too much to bear. He believed Aggie had loved him, but she always put the military's needs first. The army took precedence over everything, including their relationship.

"Thanks for the update. I guess we'll have to keep looking." He and Oz kept a low profile and worked on the case during off hours. Bronson vowed to never give up until he knew the truth about Corbin's death and his partner promised to support him through the entire process. Maybe finding answers would bring him some peace one day.

Until then, he had a job to do. And he wouldn't shirk that duty, no matter how he felt about seeing Aggie again.

"Can you meet me at Sal's Diner? Aggie Newton's sister's been abducted."

"Absolutely. I'm on my way."

"Bring the FOIA document, too. I want to see it."

"Will do."

Bronson ended the call and pulled into the restaurant parking lot. The small diner was one of twelve shops in the strip mall off Main Street. The area was typically safe and bustling with patrons on a Saturday afternoon, but the growing crowd of curious onlookers didn't help to preserve the crime scene.

Yellow tape circled a small area around a red sedan with North Carolina plates, but Aggie had mentioned a white van leaving the lot and that area wasn't included inside the perimeter.

Bronson parked his car, signed the crime scene login sheet, and approached one of his colleagues.

"Hey, Troy. How about we extend our boundary all the way to the road and block off the entrances? We don't need more people coming in here. Also, can we get a few officers to push these people back a bit?"

"Will do, Detective, but these business owners aren't going to be happy that we're cutting off their customers."

"If they have a problem with it, then send them to me, otherwise, rope this off."

"Yes, sir."

Bronson scanned the area. "By the way, any idea where Aggie Newton is?"

"She took her niece inside."

"Thanks."

Bronson headed up the hill and stepped into the entrance of Sal's Diner. Country music and the scent of grilled meat tempted him to order a cheeseburger to go. He'd been busy catching up on paperwork all morning and hadn't eaten lunch.

Servers bustled around the space and delivered trays of fried foods to tables of hungry customers. Sal's massive collection of antique model cars decorated every nook and gave the place a fifties vibe.

Aggie sat in a red vinyl booth near the window, running her thumb along the rim of a mug. Steam rose into the air. Probably hot tea, her favorite. She raised her green-eyed glassy gaze to his when he approached and had never looked more tortured with grief in all the years he'd known her.

She smoothed her fingers through her niece's dark hair, the same shade as her own. Holly rested her head against Aggie's arm and folded a flattened plastic straw into squares.

"That's going to get cold if you don't drink it," he said, hoping to lessen any awkwardness between them.

She forced a sad smile to her face and motioned to the seat across from her. "Thanks for coming."

"Of course." He slid across the vinyl and waited for her to collect herself.

She lifted the mug to her lips, swallowed a sip and then placed it on the table again, staring into the dark liquid as if all the answers to her problems lived there. "You'll be the one to work this case, correct?"

"I've asked my sergeant to assign this one to me and my partner, Oz." He placed a hand on her arm. "I'm so sorry you're going through this. Any idea who took her?"

She looked at his hand on her arm but didn't move away from his touch. "I don't know."

"We need to go over everything that happened while your memory is still fresh."

"Of course." She pulled a napkin from the dispenser and dabbed the corners of her eyes, while he pulled out his notebook and pen.

"Are you home on leave?" he asked.

"I'm home for good."

He paused. "You discharged?"

She nodded.

"But I thought you planned to stay in the army until you retired."

"Things change." She stared into her mug again. "It was time to come home."

A response escaped him, but the memories of all the arguments they had about her military career still sat fresh in his memory. He redirected his thoughts back to the task at hand. "Tell me what happened today."

"I hired a moving company to pack up and move my belongings from the base, not that I had much." She took another sip of tea. "Instead of driving, I treated myself to a first-class flight home."

"Well-deserved."

"Leslie picked me up from the airport and we came straight here to appease my craving for Sal's lasagna—a small celebration before the large party my mom had planned." She shook her head. "Now, I just keep thinking, if we hadn't stopped, then she'd still be here."

"This isn't your fault. We'll find her."

"Who would take her? She's a housewife and mother. She doesn't have a bad bone in her body."

"The details will help us find answers. You had lunch, then what happened?"

"Leslie and Holly decided to go to the car while I paid the bill."

Holly sat up. Wide green eyes looked at him—Aggie's eyes, and Leslie's as well, given that the sisters were twins. He remembered the little girl from a few family gatherings at the apple farm.

"Mommy buckled me into my seat. Then a man at the door grabbed her. She tried to fight him off, but another man helped hold her still. He pulled her into the van."

"That's great, Holly. Do you remember what he looked like?"

"He was wearing a sweatshirt with a hood."

"Did you see his face?"

The little girl looked down. "He had black bushy eyebrows and mean eyes."

Bronson jotted the information into his notepad.

"They called her Aggie."

They both straightened at the girl's revelation.

"Are you sure he said my name, sweetie?" Aggie asked.

Holly nodded.

"Did your mom correct him? Tell him her name was Leslie?"

"I don't think so." The little girl blinked a

couple of times, fighting back the tears threatening to spill down her cheeks.

Holly's statement alarmed him. If they took Leslie by mistake, then Aggie was the real target. "I know you and your sister are twins, but I've always been able to tell you two apart. You dress and wear your hair different."

"She was wearing my coat," Aggie said. "I gave it to her so she could wrap it around Holly to keep her warm. She promised to heat the car up for me. When I came out, she was gone. They thought she was me. I'm the target, not her."

"Why would someone want to take you?" Bronson asked.

She kept circling her thumb along the edge of the mug. "I have no idea."

"What about the van? Did you see it?"

"It was white and ran another car off the road when it pulled into the street. I didn't see the license plate, though."

"We need to figure out why they wanted you. You're not safe until we understand what they're after."

Holly hugged onto Aggie's arm tighter. "They aren't going to take you, too, are they, Aunt Aggie?"

She stroked her fingers through her niece's hair. "Of course not."

Bronson glanced out the window and surveyed the roofline of the restaurant. "Looks like Sal's got some security cameras in place. Let's hope they're working and have a reliable recording."

"Aggie?" An older woman entered the diner and moved toward them. Bronson recognized her as Aggie's mother. She had the same slender figure, dark hair, and green eyes as her daughters.

"Did you call her?" Aggie asked him.

"Wasn't me." Bronson slid over to make room for the woman.

"Mom, I was going to call you—"

"A neighbor called and told me what she'd heard." She sat and looked at Bronson. "Is it true? Did someone take Leslie?"

"We have the Mills Creek police looking for her, Mrs. Newton."

Her mother's fingers flew to her lips as she fought back the tears filling her eyes. "Who would take my daughter?"

"Maybe we should talk about this later, away from little ears." Aggie pointed to Holly.

The six-year-old sat up again. "Hey, my ears aren't little."

Bronson fought back a smile at Holly's statement, but the urgency of their situation overshadowed any amusement.

"You'll bring Leslie home, right?" Aggie's mother asked.

"Investigators are working to collect as much evidence as possible. Do you know of anyone who would want to take Leslie or Aggie?"

"Aggie? Are they after her, too?"

"Of course not, Mom." Aggie placed a hand on the woman's arm and shot Bronson a look. One he'd seen before when they dated, and she wanted him to stop talking. "Why don't you take Holly home? She's exhausted. I can stay with Bronson in case he needs me to answer any more questions."

"Is that okay if I take my granddaughter home? Or would it be better if we both stayed here?"

"That's fine," he said. "Investigators will be coming to the farm to collect any evidence of Leslie's that might help them find her. If anyone contacts you regarding her whereabouts or if you think of anything that you believe might help, don't hesitate to call." He slid one of his cards across the table.

Aggie leaned close to Holly's ear, whispered a few words and then her niece reached for her grandmother. "I'll be home later. Keep her with you and don't let her out of your sight."

The older woman hugged her granddaughter

close and looked at Bronson over the little girl's shoulder. "Please find my daughter."

He usually didn't make promises, but this was an exception. He had to find Leslie. "We will, Mrs. Newton."

While Aggie escorted her mother to their car, Bronson sent a couple of units to follow the same route the van took when leaving the diner. "Canvas the entire area within a ten-mile radius. Actually, scratch that. Go all the way to the city limit. Find this van for me."

Bronson met Aggie as they both headed back into the diner. He held the door open for her. "Want to view the security footage with me?"

"I thought you'd never ask."

Sal Costa, a short, dark-headed man with a handlebar mustache, motioned them down a hallway and into his office. Multiple monitors lined the back of the room.

"I can't believe someone would do this, here in Mills Creek, of all places. Especially outside my diner." Sal clicked several buttons and found the desired footage.

Bronson pointed to the screen. "Right there. Hit play."

The events rolled across the screen as Holly had described but the camera's angle did not allow for a view of the abductors' faces. Leslie fought hard and almost escaped their attack, but the two men succeeded in loading her into the van. He'd worked abduction cases like this before. They were often organized and didn't end with a positive outcome.

"Can you zoom up on that license plate?"

Sal dragged a digital box over the area of interest. The combination of letters and numbers enlarged but only the first two identifiers were recognizable.

"H and T. That gives us something to go on," Aggie said.

Bronson handed the man one of the USB drives he kept in his jacket pocket. "Can you save me a copy? I'll have my cyber team clean it up."

"Sure, no problem." Sal pushed the device into his computer, tapped a couple of keys, then handed it back to Bronson when the download finished.

"Did you or any of your staff see anything?"

"I've questioned them all, but this happened during our lunch rush, and we were slammed. Did no one else in the parking lot see anything?"

"We've got officers questioning a few bystanders, but the car was parked beside a large box truck which helped hide what was happening."

"If only I'd chosen a different space," Aggie said.

Bronson touched her hand. "Don't do that.

This is not your fault. They would've carried out the abduction no matter where you parked. Did you notice if anyone followed you from the airport?"

"Not that I saw."

"Did you look?"

"I'm a soldier who's been deployed six times to Afghanistan. Of course, I looked. Every time I go into a restaurant, I sit with my back to the wall, facing the door. I know the number of people in the room, how many servers are on the floor and if anyone has a backpack or large purse beside them. I scope out all the exits and decide which one I'll take if needed, all before the waitress brings my water."

His brother had been the same way when he returned home after his first deployment. He assessed every situation for potential threats when they were in public places and hated to be in crowds.

"What about when you got here for lunch? Did you notice anyone watching you?"

"Palmer Sterling." She slipped her fingers into her pocket and handed Bronson a business card. "He approached me when I was waiting to pay."

He read the card. "The CEO of Sterling Securities? Sal's diner's not really his scene."

Sal swiveled around in his chair. "Hey. I'll

have you know I have many wealthy people eat at my restaurant."

"Sorry, Sal. Didn't mean to offend." Bronson squeezed the man's shoulder and turned his attention back to Aggie. "What did Sterling want?"

"He offered me a job."

"A job?"

"He needs a helicopter pilot."

"But you're not taking it, right?" Sterling's reputation was cutthroat—and more than a little shady. Seemed like his name always cropped up in multiple cases, but they were never able to officially tie him to anything criminal. Sterling liked his high-paying private military contracts and would do anything just shy of illegal to keep them.

"I came home to help Mom with the apple farm, not work the skies anymore."

"Good. Sterling Securities is not the place for you."

Her body stiffened next to him. "Why do you say that? You don't think my skills measure up?"

"Your skills are fine, I'm sure. Sterling has some questionable ethics. That's all."

"I've heard the rumors, but I can take care of myself. I'm fully capable of working for Sterling Securities and keeping my integrity."

"Of course," he said, aware of the sudden strain between them. Her stubborn streak was another hurdle they'd struggled to overcome in their relationship. He wanted a partner who would work on life with him. Someone who would consider his opinions as valid.

Sal stood from his chair, interrupting the tense moment. "Let me fix you some food." He motioned back toward the dining room. "You can take it home for your family tonight."

"Thanks, Sal. Mom would appreciate that."

Bronson took the man's seat and rewound the footage to watch again. "If we're going to find your sister, then we can't let our personal issues get in the way."

She leaned over his shoulder, circulating a wisp of fresh vanilla-scented perfume. "I agree. I wouldn't have called you if I didn't think you were the best person to help me find her."

"Thanks." He paused the video. "His sleeve is pushed up when he gets back in the van on the passenger side. See that?"

"Part of a tattoo?"

"I'll have my cybersecurity team clean up the image and see if we can get a better visual. Might be a way to identify the man."

Sal returned, holding two large bags filled with food. "Here you are, my sweet Agatha. We've got lasagna, salad, some of my special garlic bread, and a side of ravioli stuffed with four different kinds of cheeses. This will last for several days."

Bronson never heard anyone call Aggie by her full name. She leaned in and gave Sal a hug and then took the bags from him. "Thank you."

"My pleasure. I hope this brings your mother comfort." The man fought back tears rimming his eyes. "I'm so sorry you're going through this."

She hugged him again. "We're going to be okay. We'll find Leslie. This food will definitely bring us comfort."

Bronson stood and pulled his keys from his pocket. "You can put all that in my SUV if you want. I just need to do a couple more things, and then I can take you home."

"I've got my sister's car."

Bronson shook his head. "We need to hold her car for evidence."

"Right. I wasn't thinking."

He motioned toward the hallway. "After you."

They exited Sal's diner and Bronson opened the vehicle's door for her to put the food inside. Then he motioned toward the road. "Do you mind showing me the exact route the van took?"

"Won't that be on the police report?"

"Yeah, but sometimes seeing the scene first-hand can help."

They walked in silence for a few moments.

Bronson replayed the evidence in his head. "Your sister was wearing your coat and your niece heard them say your name. Why do you think they want you?"

"Still thinking that through."

"You just discharged from the army and haven't even made it home yet. Don't you think this could all be tied to something from your military past?"

She hesitated for a moment and looked across the parking lot. "Maybe, but I really can't say for sure."

He studied her. "I find that hard to believe. There's got to be something to—"

"Trust me. I've been racking my brain since Holly told me they said my name. Shouldn't we be looking at Leslie, too? Maybe this really is about her." She swiped away a stray hair from her cheek.

"Okay. What about Leslie? Anyone you know who might want to hurt her?"

"Maybe her ex—Holly's father. They've been divorced now for six months because of his violent temper. He left town and she thought she was rid of him, but Leslie said he showed up the other night wanting to see Holly, promising he was a changed man."

"Did your sister believe him?"

"She told him to leave. They've got a restraining order against him, and he can't come within fifty yards of Leslie or his daughter."

"What's his name?"

"Tony Keene."

"I'll run his name through our database, but I'll be honest, the timing indicates you're more likely to be the target than your sister. Especially with your military background."

Bronson stepped onto the sidewalk that ran adjacent to Main Street. Few cars were out tonight with the temperature dropping into the forties after sunset. Dimmed headlights passed by on occasion and Bronson had to use his phone's flashlight to search the area. His beam caught a reflection and he halted traffic to inspect remnants of orange plastic pieces littering the asphalt. He collected the debris and made his way back to where Aggie stood.

"What is it?" she asked.

"Looks like your sister busted out a taillight."

She smiled. "That's my girl."

Lights behind her brightened, almost blinding Bronson. Tires squealed and a large vehicle veered off the road headed straight for them. With no time to speak, Bronson grabbed Aggie by the shoulders and tackled her to the ground. A rush of wind blew past them, while metal crunched, and gravel rained across their bodies. He covered their heads with his arms and prayed they didn't get hit.

TWO

The engine revved as bystanders screamed and jumped out of the vehicle's way. Diesel fumes and black soot from the rusted truck's extended tail pipes dusted Bronson's skin. Debris pelted the side of his face as he looked up.

The word "Rattitude" decorated the door in an array of colors. He tried to get a look at the driver, but white smoke from squalling tires obscured his vision. Nearby officers ran to their cars, activated their blue lights, and pursued the reckless driver.

Aggie coughed beneath him. Her eyes were still shut and her full lips too close to his, triggering the memory of their last kiss—the one that had come during the fight that ended their relationship.

Long black lashes fluttered opened, and Aggie's green eyes stared back at him. "Are you okay?"

"Yeah. Are you?" He wiped a smudge of dirt

from her cheek, her skin soft beneath his finger. She placed a hand to his chest and pushed him back.

"I'm good."

He rolled to a seated position next to her. "Sorry. I didn't mean to tackle you."

"There wasn't much time, and it was the only way to keep me from getting hit." She stood and extended a hand to help him to his feet. "There's black soot all over your clothes."

He brushed his fingers across his pants. "Nothing a little laundry detergent can't fix."

"Did you get a look at the driver?"

"Not really. Our patrol units will get him."

"You think he just lost control?" she asked.

"Not sure. Could be a rubbernecker not paying attention to the road because of all the blue lights in the parking area. We see it all the time with crime scenes or highway accidents. Either way, we'll know more once the officers pull him over. In the meantime, just to be safe, I think we need to set a rotating patrol at your house until we have a better idea of what's going on."

She removed a hair tie from her pocket and pulled dark strands into a ponytail. "I'm a trained soldier. I can take care of myself and my family. Please focus on finding my sister. I'll be fine."

"Are you sure about that?" He pointed at the back of her forearm, drawing attention to a two-inch gash deep enough to need stitches. "Might want the paramedics to take care of that for you, unless you can do that yourself, too."

His words came out harsher than he intended, but her tough attitude could get frustrating at times. She wasn't in the military anymore with a platoon of soldiers around to keep her safe. Killers played by a different set of rules. In a situation like this, he was the one with expertise and had closed more cases than any other detective in their unit this year. A little respect for his experience would be nice.

He turned up the volume on his radio. "Reckless driver apprehended. Sixteen-year-old male with four friends in his rat rod of a truck. Received his license a week ago. States he got distracted when he saw the crime scene and ran off the road."

Bronson clicked his talk switch. "Ten-four. Thanks for the update."

He held up the bag of evidence and gave the pieces inside a little shake, then looked back to Aggie who swiped the cut with her palm. "I'll be with the investigators. The paramedic is over there. Might want to get them to clean that before they're released to another scene or before it gets infected."

She heeded his advice and headed to the ambulance, while he approached a group of three officers studying a map of Mills Creek, stretched across the back of one of their SUVs. Bronson placed the baggy of broken taillight pieces in front of them. "Found these in the road. I want to know if they're from our van."

A female investigator dumped the pieces onto the carpeted tailgate and fitted them back together. "I've got one of these at home. Well, actually, two on the back of my van. These lights are from a 2015 to 2019 Ford Transit van. I know that because I had to replace mine when some teenage driver rear-ended me after ridin' my tail too close. That matches the make and model seen leaving the crime scene on the security footage."

"Are you sure?"

"Without a doubt."

Bronson clicked his radio again. "Update on our white Ford Transit van. The vehicle is between a 2015 and a 2019 model. It also has a broken taillight on the driver's side, rear."

Two police cars left the scene to help with the search, while the number of onlookers continued to increase. He'd hoped pushing out the crime scene tape would keep the curious away, but the word must've spread around the neighborhood. The press would be here soon, and he needed to get a photo of Leslie for them to broadcast. He texted Aggie for an updated picture.

After a few minutes, the unit's call came back. "Officer, 287-Adam. We have your van. It's empty. They ditched it."

"Any evidence there to tell us what they drove to escape?"

"We've got an eyewitness that saw a gray Chevy truck parked there around the same time as our abduction. There are some tire tracks here that don't match the van's. I'll have one of the investigators see if they fit the truck."

Bronson's hope faded. By switching vehicles, the intruders made finding Leslie harder, but if they matched the tire treads to the truck, then that would help. If only Holly could remember the abductor's faces…but recalling them might be too much for a six-year-old to handle. He couldn't blame her for not noticing many details. She was bound to be traumatized after everything she'd experienced.

"Are we sure the van is the one used in our victim's abduction?"

"White Ford Transit with a broken driver's side taillight. This is the one."

"What about the license plate?"

"There isn't one. They must've taken the tag with them."

"Copy," Bronson said.

"One more thing." Static filtered through the radio. "We've found evidence of blood in the back. You might want to see this in person."

"How much?"

"Trace amounts. Onsite test results came back human, and the lab will be able to get DNA once they have the sample. Got some strands of dark hair, too, and a few silver charms."

"Did he say silver?" a female voice asked. Bronson turned and Aggie stood behind him with her arm bandaged.

"Yeah. Why?"

"I gave Leslie a silver charm bracelet last year for Christmas. She was wearing it today."

Bronson pressed the talk button again. "Send me the GPS coordinates. I'm on my way."

"I'm going with you," Aggie said.

He needed to focus on his job if he wanted to find her sister as quickly as possible. Her presence would be a distraction. "You need to go home and be with your family."

"No way. I'm going with you."

He walked faster. "I know this is my issue, but I'll work better without my ex-fiancée around. Our main goal is to find Leslie ASAP, so, it would be best if you went home and supported your mom and Holly."

"It's not easy for me to be around you, either,

but she's my sister. If this was your brother, wouldn't you want to be involved?"

He stopped and faced her. "I can't believe you just asked me that."

Aggie looked out at the road, her lips pressed together into a thin line. "I know. You're right. I shouldn't—"

"It's only been a year. Surely you've not forgotten."

"My apologies. I wasn't thinking."

He twisted his brother's gold-plated key ring around his finger. The piece, engraved with Corbin's infantry number, had been a gift from Bronson for completing boot camp. When the army delivered Corbin's personal effects after his death, Bronson found his gift in the box and carried the memento with him every day.

She was right about one thing. If his brother were still alive, Bronson would do anything to protect him. Whatever his grudge was against Aggie, he knew she felt just as strongly about her sister. He didn't want her around, but he nodded toward the passenger door anyway. "Get in but do exactly as I say."

Bronson took his seat in the SUV and rolled down his driver's side window when his partner, Detective Oz Kelly, pulled up beside him.

"Need another set of eyes?"

"Couldn't hurt." Bronson started his vehicle,

fell in behind Oz and activated his blue lights in hopes that most traffic would move aside.

Aggie adjusted her seat. "You're right."

"You doubted?"

"I guess there's a first time for everything," she shot back.

He maneuvered through a red light with caution. "What am I right about?"

"I was the intended target. Not my sister. That's the only theory that makes any sense."

He couldn't disagree. He only hoped Leslie didn't pay the ultimate price when her attackers discovered they had the wrong sister.

Raindrops blew onto the main farmhouse porch and sprayed against Aggie's soaked clothes as well as the plastic bag holding her only comfort for the night—Sal's lasagna. After searching for evidence in the pouring rain, she planned to eat a large helping or maybe two.

The deluge from earlier had managed to drench all the officers at the abandoned lot, but they didn't give up when it came to gathering as much evidence as possible. At the first sprinkles, they erected tents to preserve what they could and continued to work for at least another hour, gathering evidence before more washed away. She'd hoped the blood in the van would identify the men who took her sister and provide a lead, but in her heart, she knew it was far more likely that the trace amounts belonged to Leslie.

A flash of lightning brightened the sky and triggered a rumble of thunder. At least the storm would drown out any noise she was making. She didn't want to wake her mother or Holly, who both appeared to have retired for the night.

Aggie fumbled with her keys and jabbed one into the lock. When the door didn't open, she thumped her head against the glass, frustrated with herself that she couldn't even manage this. She felt like such a failure. They were no closer to finding Leslie. What was she going to tell her mother? How could she admit that if Aggie had stayed away, Leslie would be in her own home tonight, safe and sound?

She straightened her shoulders, wiped the wetness from her cheeks and tried the lock again. The door finally clicked open just as headlights from an approaching vehicle brightened the porch. Aggie placed the food on an entry table, pulled the door closed and stepped to the edge, ignoring the whips of rain.

The black sedan stopped in front of her, and a man jumped out. "Where's Holly? Is she okay? I heard about the abduction."

Tony Keene, Holly's father, walked toward her, his eyes widened with a look of fear. Aggie glanced back at the house. "Keep your voice down. Holly and my mother are asleep."

"I want to see her. I want to see Holly."

"First off, that's not going to happen tonight because I'm not dragging her out of her bed for anything but an emergency. Second, you're violating the restraining order Leslie has against you. However, considering the circumstances, I'll overlook the last infraction as long as you hop back in your car and mosey on out of here."

Tony raked his hands into his dark, curly hair and paced in front of the porch steps. "I just need to know she's okay. She's my daughter, too, Aggie."

She folded her arms across her chest to fight off the shivers from her wet clothing. "You should've remembered that before you hit my sister."

"That was a mistake and I've never laid a hand on Holly. You know that."

"I do."

He continued pacing and remained under the roofline to keep from the rain. "I've been going to counseling, I've been sober for six months and I've got a job now—a steady one. I know it's going to take time, but I want a relationship with my daughter. Tonight, I just need to know if Holly's okay."

His emotional distress deepened the lines on his forehead. He'd been a good guy at one time, before he'd let alcohol take over. Aggie hoped what he said about turning over a new leaf was true. Holly often asked about her father and wanted to see him, but after all they'd been through tonight, she couldn't add to her niece's trauma. "She's fine. Upset about her mother, but physically unscathed."

His arms dropped to his side and his shoulders sagged. He leaned against the porch railing, rainwater dripping from every inch of him. "Will you tell her I love her and give her a letter for me?"

"You know I don't like being in the middle of your—"

"It's just a letter. Leslie usually gives them to her when I mail them each week and I don't want her to miss one. Please, Aggie. I want her to know I'm here for her, especially when she's going through the roughest time of her life."

The sooner she cooperated, the sooner he'd leave and she could go inside to get warm. He always did have a way of using someone else's discomfort to his advantage.

She held out her hand and Tony rushed back to the car, rummaged around, and then returned with a crumpled-up envelope. Holly's name was scribbled on the outside. "Thanks for this.

We've got a supervised visit scheduled for next week. Tell her I can't wait to see her."

Aggie nodded, not sure she wanted to over-burden Holly with more stress while they searched for her mother. Hopefully, they'd have Leslie back by then and she could make the decision. Tony slipped back into his car and drove away.

With him gone, Aggie rushed inside, grabbed a pair of dry fatigues from her army duffel, changed in the downstairs bathroom, and then made her way to the kitchen.

Scents of cinnamon and nutmeg welcomed her into the room. "Surely, she didn't," Aggie said as she opened the pantry door. A container of cookies sat on the top shelf. Oatmeal raisin, her sister's favorite. "I guess she did."

Her mother's footsteps shuffled into the kitchen from the hallway. When Aggie turned to face her, she saw that her eyes were puffy and red. She usually looked younger than her age of sixty-five, but the stress of Leslie's disappearance had already taken a toll.

"Did they find her?" Her mother leaned against the quartz countertop.

"Not yet." Aggie grabbed a napkin from the holder and popped a chunk of cookie in her mouth. "Did you bake these today? After everything with Leslie?"

Her mom folded her arms across her chest, jaw tightening, tears pooling in her eyes again. "Holly wanted some and after all that poor little girl has been through today, I'd bake her a wedding cake if she asked. Besides, it kept my mind busy and hers. I couldn't just sit here and…"

Her words faded into sobs. Aggie pulled her mother into a hug and mentally scolded herself for questioning the woman's coping mechanisms. Personally, Aggie would rather shoot up a target or hit a punching bag, but her mom handled her grief with plates of homemade cookies and fresh baked apple pie—her late father's favorite.

"We're going to find Leslie." Aggie pulled back. "How's Holly?"

"Sleeping. I gave her Leslie's old stuffed bear from when she was a little girl. Holly curled up on the couch a couple of hours ago and conked out. I moved her to Leslie's old bedroom for the night. Your room's ready, too. Fresh sheets and an extra quilt. This storm's brought in quite a chill." Her mother fingered a strand of her wet hair. "Did you not wear your raincoat with the hood?"

"It wouldn't really help anyway. The wind was whipping, and we all got soaked despite the tents." Aggie took another bite of cookie, not wanting to acknowledge the guilt of giving

Leslie her coat. "What happened to Mr. Cuddles, the teddy bear Holly likes to sleep with?"

Another round of tears sprung to her mother's eyes. "I couldn't handle the thought of going into Leslie's house to get it. I knew if I walked inside…"

She didn't finish her sentence. With age, the loss of their father and now Leslie's disappearance, her mother's resolve had withered.

"Bronson and his team are some of the best detectives in the state. They've got a patrol team canvasing the area for her tonight and he promised me an update first thing in the morning."

"What if they don't find her? Or worse, what if they do and she's hurt or—"

"Let's not think the worst." Aggie wanted to keep her mom's thoughts positive. "He's going to find her and bring her home, safe and sound."

Her mother dug into the pocket of her pink terrycloth bathrobe, retrieved a used tissue and wiped her eyes. "I've got to stop crying. That doesn't help Leslie or Holly in any way."

"I think a mother's allowed a few tears when something traumatic happens to her daughter. I'll go over tomorrow and get Holly's things. Make me a list so I don't forget anything." She finished off the cookie, the only thing she'd eaten since her lunch with her sister, and filled a plate with Sal's lasagna.

"Want some? Sal sent it for us."

"That's sweet but not right now. Maybe tomorrow."

Aggie pulled her phone from her pocket while the food heated in the microwave. "Bronson said he'd text if anything new developed tonight. I'll keep you posted since I'm sure that neither of us will be able to sleep much."

"I'd appreciate that. I just want her home without a scratch on her."

"You and me both."

Her mother motioned to the dining room table. "By the way, these came for you today."

Aggie turned. A gorgeous bouquet of pink tulips in a green glass vase sat on the table. "Wow. Those are beautiful. Who are they from?"

"I don't know. I didn't look."

She read the card. *"Hoping your journey home leads you to our company."* Aggie flipped the card over. "They're from Palmer Sterling, the CEO of Sterling Securities."

"Why would he be sending you flowers?"

"I saw him at the diner today. He offered me a job as a helicopter pilot."

"He was there?"

"Yeah. The timing was a bit odd. I told him I was going to be working on our farm with you."

"And where was Leslie when you were talking with him?"

"She and Holly had gone to the car."

"You don't think—"

"Not at all. He was nice. I'm sure he had nothing to do with Leslie's disappearance."

"But still. A CEO of a fortune five hundred company eating in a small-town diner? That seems a bit unusual."

"Yeah. It is a bit odd. He said he grew up in a small town and comes north to Mills Creek to eat lunch when he needs driving time to think."

"You must've had quite a chat with him."

Suspicion rang through her mother's tone. She sounded just the way she had when Aggie was in high school and dated a guy her mother didn't like. "Can you believe someone told him I was one of the best helicopter pilots in the area?"

"Not a surprise to me. You've always been an overachiever."

"Still. There are so many other pilots better than I am. I think it was his way of trying to butter me up to take the job."

"Don't sell yourself short. I doubt he would be so interested in hiring you unless plenty of people vouched for your reputation. Is this something you want to do? I don't want the farm or me to hold you back from an opportunity."

"Maybe in the future, but the timing is off right now. I can't go traipsing after a new career, especially with Leslie missing. Plus, I just got home and want to work here. Spend some time with you and our family."

Her mother wrapped an arm around her shoulders. "What would I do without you?"

"You've been without me for ten years and this place is running like clockwork. I think you'd do just fine."

"That's not what I mean, and you know it. This farm has always been for you and Leslie. Your sister made sure everything ran smoothly. I barely had to lift a finger."

"And I'm here to help with those things now, too."

"Well, right now, the best use of your skills will be finding your sister. You have military training and hostage recovery experience that will benefit the cops. We have to find her."

Aggie placed a hand over her mother's. "We will."

"With you and Bronson working together, I have no doubt our Leslie will be back home with us soon. Was it good to see him again?"

"Not sure good is the right word. Maybe different or awkward would be better."

Her mother walked to the sink and grabbed a sponge to wipe up the few crumbs Aggie left behind from her cookie. "Oh, nonsense. You always did have a special chemistry together. I'm still shocked the two of you weren't able to work out your differences."

"Hard to work out an issue you're forbidden to discuss." She still struggled with her part in Corbin's death, but when the army labeled something classified, a secret was born. She just never thought those secrets would drive away her fiancé.

Aggie filled a glass with some water and took a sip. "You know I'll do everything I can to bring Leslie home, but I want to prepare you. Sometimes we don't get the outcome we want."

"I have to believe we will in this case. God will bring her back to us. Use the skills He's given you and trust Him to bring your sister home. Once she's back, you can move on to bigger things like Sterling." Her mother returned the sponge to the sink and pointed at the flowers. "Although, I don't think I've ever heard of a CEO of a company wooing a potential employee with flowers."

"Yeah." Aggie crossed back to the vase, bent her head forward and sniffed one of the bulbs. "Me, either."

The gesture raised red flags in the back of

Aggie's mind, but maybe she was jaded from her time in the military. Over there, everyone was a suspect—a potential attacker with an ulterior motive. The move back home and adjusting to a civilian mindset might take more work than she first expected, but she didn't have to figure everything out tonight.

Aggie finished eating, rinsed her plate and with a kiss to her mother's cheek, she lifted her bag to her shoulder and headed upstairs to her room. "I'm beat. Going to bed. Love you."

"Love you, too."

Her room still held faded scents of perfume and hairspray lingering in the beige carpet from her teenage years. Light pink hues decorated the walls and plantation blinds covered the windows.

Her four-poster bed sat against the opposite wall positioned to expose the mountain views. An extensive book collection remained on the shelves, organized by color. Her mother left the leather-bound Bible on her nightstand opened to her favorite verse. She smiled at the steady consistency of home and soaked in its comfort despite the chaos in her life.

Aggie plopped on the bed, pulled a laptop from her bag, and opened her email inbox. A message from Sterling Securities' human resource manager sat bolded in the sidebar. Apparently, they'd been watching her military career for years, were impressed by her accomplishments and had matched her to the listed qualifications. She clicked a second attachment and was stunned at the job offer—two hundred and fifty thousand the first year. That amount took her almost three years to make in the military. She had until close of the business week to respond.

Something about Sterling's pushiness unnerved her. They'd been able to uncover private details about her career and even though they were the top security firm in the area, their moves felt intrusive, like they had her under surveillance.

Aggie propped a pillow behind her back when the backyard light spilled through the slats of her window's plantation blinds.

She stilled for a moment. Waiting.

Probably a stray dog or cat on a nighttime prowl.

But the glow continued.

Her father said he installed the instant spotlight for security back in the day, but she and Leslie knew the real reason was to ward off any undesirable teenage boyfriends.

But there were no boyfriends visiting tonight and Aggie pushed her laptop to the side, moved to the window and lifted the blinds. A gray truck crept up the mile-long drive and pulled to the edge, the continuous wisp of exhaust smoke triggering the motion sensor. Shadows moved inside the cab, but no one ever emerged.

The bowtie on the grill and emblem on the side confirmed the brand—a Chevy Silverado. The same make and model the eyewitness spotted at the abandoned lot. It couldn't be a coincidence.

Enough with the scare tactics. She wasn't going to let these people intimidate her. Aggie crept down the stairs and opened the front closet, her fingers searching the top shelf for the long barrel of her father's rifle. If they wanted to mess with the ones she loved, then she'd make sure they regretted ever stepping foot on her family's land.

THREE

Bronson wound down the gravel drive to the Newton family home. The rain had stopped but rolls of thunder continued to rumble across the sky. His truck splashed through a couple of puddled ruts.

He'd sent Aggie home from the abandoned lot about an hour ago, knowing she needed some rest. The stress of traveling home and the trauma of her sister's abduction had taken a toll. He hoped she was able to get some sleep, but knowing Aggie, that was doubtful.

He tapped Oz's number. "Any news on the abductors? Did they call with a ransom?"

"I checked with our team earlier. Nothing yet."

"If they don't want money, then the abduction is probably about intel they want from Aggie—or maybe payback for one of her missions."

"Could be, but let's not jump to conclusions.

We'll figure out their motive. We have to keep looking."

Oz sounded tired.

"Why don't you get some sleep? We can start first thing in the morning."

"I may catch a few hours here in a bit, but I've had about three cups of coffee and couldn't go to sleep if I wanted."

They traded a few more tidbits of information and ended the call with little progress made. Bronson rounded a curve in Aggie's driveway and spotted a reflection through the trees. A truck was parked a hundred yards from the main house against a row of evergreens. Bronson cut his lights before topping the small hill and pulled his SUV to the side of the road. He couldn't tell if anyone was in the vehicle and needed a closer look.

He crept along the tree line, his gun in hand, and remained in the shadows despite the bright outside lights in Aggie's yard. The truck was gray. A Chevy Silverado, like the eyewitness described. Tinted windows kept him from viewing any faces, but shadows moved inside the cab.

Bronson sprinted from the woods to the back tailgate. The license plate read HTX-335, the same first two letters from the diner's security footage. They must've switched the van's plates to the Silverado.

He called for backup, then moved to the driver's side rear wheel. The overgrown woods and his black hoodie provided enough darkness to keep him camouflaged.

A screen door creaked open. Aggie stepped onto the porch, her boots thumping across the wooden surface with purpose as she darted toward the thick, stone corner post. Her family's German shepherd, McIntosh, was at her heels, barking with a vengeance.

She commanded him to stay by her side and aimed an M1 carbine rifle at the truck but didn't fire. "You need to leave. I've called 911."

Two shots erupted from the truck in Aggie's direction. She took cover, then pivoted her position and returned fire. No hesitation. Fifteen shots. The bullets pinged off the truck's hood. Not bad from the long distance of the porch.

Bronson ducked and headed for cover, to the rear of the truck, but the engine cranked to life. White backup lights flashed on, and he dove for the bushes as the truck hit the gas in reverse. They almost ran over him, trying to avoid Aggie's reloaded onslaught.

She pivoted into view and aimed the barrel right at the driver. Gravel and dust spun into the air, creating a smoke screen. She pulled the trigger.

The front tire blew.

The windshield shattered.

Bronson raised his Glock and fired as well, but the truck escaped.

He shoved his gun into his side holster, raised his arms and faced Aggie. She stood on the porch with her rifle still aimed at the road. When she saw his face emerge from the shadows, she dropped the barrel to the ground. "What are you doing here? I could've shot you."

"I appreciate your restraint." He motioned back down the driveway. "How long were they here?"

"Not sure. I saw them out my window and didn't want them near Holly or my mom."

"I think they got the message."

"You didn't answer my question."

He walked up to the edge of the porch steps where she stood, thankful to see she was unscathed from the opposing gunfire. "I was doing a security check and saw the gray truck parked on your road."

"Matches the description the eyewitness gave at the abandoned lot."

"Looks that way."

"They must know they have my sister instead of me. That's not good."

Bronson walked onto the porch and leaned against one of the railings. "Maybe. Or they'll use her as leverage."

"Great. Just what I want to hear. I wish they'd contact us instead of lurking."

The screen door pushed open, and Mrs. Newton stepped onto the porch behind them. "What in the world is going on?"

"We had an intruder. Did Holly wake up?" Aggie asked, handing the rifle to her mother.

"I don't know how she didn't, but that little one slept right through all the racket. Maybe she thought it was thunder from the storm. Are they gone?"

"For now." Aggie nodded toward her sister's house. "While I'm up, I might as well head over to Leslie's place and pick up Holly's teddy bear and some clothes for her. Might bring her comfort when she wakes up in the morning." She motioned toward the front door. "Mom, can you hand me my cross-body bag? I placed it on the entry table."

Mrs. Newton reached inside and handed her daughter the item. "Thanks for going. Holly will love waking up with Mr. Cuddles."

Aggie slipped the strap over her head and turned toward Bronson. "Wanna walk with me?"

Fatigue was starting to set into his bones, but he fell into step beside her. They used to go for long evening walks when they dated and falling back into this familiar rhythm was nice.

The dog pushed his way in between. "Mac's always been protective of you."

"We're pretty inseparable when I'm home and he's a good guard dog. You should remember. He almost took your hand off the first time I brought you home."

"How could I forget. I think I'm still missing a chunk from my thumb."

Her hand fell to the old dog's head. "Mac and I have lost time to make up for, don't we, boy?"

Bronson leaned his head back and looked up. Stars pricked the night sky and spread above dark layered mountains looming in the distance. The stench of a skunk mixed with smoke from a distant campfire while Mills Creek babbled to the left accompanied the crunch of gravel underneath their shoes.

"We have to find her," she said.

"We will."

Aggie stopped midstride, the moon highlighting the glassiness of her eyes. "They'll kill her, Bronson. She has a daughter. How am I ever gonna explain to Holly that her mother's death is my fault? I should've never let her borrow my jacket. I can handle myself but Leslie isn't trained for this."

"She's not dead yet."

"We don't know that."

"We've got a BOLO out and every patrol on

duty is scouring the area. We're going to find her."

"We're running out of time. Twelve hours have already passed, and we aren't any closer to knowing who these people are or what they want...other than me."

"This was a planned operation. These abductors knew when you were coming home and followed you from the airport to the diner. What could they be after that would justify all the time and planning? What's their motive?"

She reached down and let her fingertips scratch Mac's head. "I don't know."

"Think. There's got to be a reason and it's probably connected to the military since that's where you've been for the last ten years."

"I left all that behind. I came home to start fresh."

"Fresh from what? You always planned to retire from the army. What changed?"

"Everything changed." She looked out over the orchards and exhaled. "I couldn't stay. Not after..."

"Not after what?"

Aggie turned away and started walking again, Mac falling into step with her. "Nothing."

The same look crossed her face as when he questioned her about Corbin's death or any other military operation.

"They'll use her for leverage to draw you out."

"Then let them. I've taken on greater threats."

"This is not Afghanistan, Aggie. You don't have an entire squad backing you up. You aren't surrounded by dozens of soldiers with weapons ready to sacrifice their lives for a team member. This is your family we're talking about."

She bent forward, picked up a stick and tossed it for Mac to retrieve. The dog took off running. "They won't get near my mother and niece. I won't let them."

"They came close tonight."

"Then we need to find them first."

Aggie took the left fork in the driveway and Bronson followed.

"They want me. Let's use that to our advantage. Set up a swap for Leslie and use me as bait."

"We don't even know who they are or what they want yet. I'm not sending you into their hands until we know why they have your sister."

"Then what's our next step? The only lead we have is a shot-up gray truck they'll probably ditch after tonight. I don't have any idea where they might've taken Leslie."

"Has anyone reached out to you, or have you had any odd encounters?"

Mac trotted back with the stick in his mouth. Aggie pulled it free and tossed it again. "Just my encounter with Palmer Sterling which I already told you about. Although, he emailed me an offer and had flowers delivered to my house."

"Sounds like he's butterin' the corn."

"You should see the salary. The amount exceeds anything I've ever seen."

Bronson wasn't thrilled with the heavy-handed tactics this company used to push her decision in their favor. "Have you met him before?"

"Not until the diner, but his company has defense contracts with the army. They supply a number of the weapons we used in the field—everything from M16s, Heckler machine guns to rocket launchers and mortar rounds. If the army paid, then Sterling Securities provided. I worked with one of their employees, named Lee Demsky. He was former military, then went to private security for the money. He's Sterling's expert in unmanned air surveillance. We used their drones to provide reconnaissance for our extractions."

"Like the one my brother's unit executed?"

She pointed up a hill, where her sister's home sat on a knoll, and smiled as Mac chased a critter back into a hole. "Exactly. Sterling Securities provides updated footage for missions and Lee would've been the one to obtain the surveillance. He's brilliant and taught me a lot about how to get good images."

"Does the drone stay in the air for the entire extraction?"

"They can if reconnaissance is needed for the entire operation. My job is to get the units in, out and back to the base with the chopper in one piece. The military often arms drones with bombs or guns to help in missions and from the heat we encountered that night, I wouldn't be surprised if Lee was engaged."

Bronson stopped walking. "Wait. You were there the night Corbin was killed?"

Her eyes widened at his question and alerted him to her slip. "There were a couple of teams carrying out the mission that night."

"You know how long I've been looking into my brother's death, and you never once told me you were their pilot. Is that why you stonewalled me when I asked you to find out the details?"

"I didn't stonewall you, Bronson." She placed her fingers to her lips and whistled for Mac to return to her side, but the dog had a scent and wasn't letting it go. "I maintained security protocols, just as I'm legally required to do. You know I have no choice."

"Yeah. I've heard that before." He took a deep breath, trying to hold on to his temper. "So Lee Demsky was with my brother's unit the night of the extraction?"

She didn't respond.

"Was he in your chopper that night or not, Aggie?" he asked again.

"What does it matter? He was on a lot of missions."

Bronson raked a hand through his hair. The only way he was going to get answers was to give her details about his case. "Because the FBI contacted us six months ago to gather evidence of criminal behavior against Sterling Securities. According to the Bureau, Palmer Sterling uses his company as a front to traffic illegal weapons, but they haven't been able to gather enough evidence to pin him to the wall."

"There's no way. Contractors are thoroughly vetted and interrogated before working with the army. Lee always followed the rules."

"How would you know for sure? By your own words, you remained in your helicopter during the missions, correct?"

"True. But I didn't see anything criminal."

"What if they thought you did?"

"Then they'd come after me."

"But grabbed Leslie instead."

They reached her sister's front steps. The

place was dark. "You really think the two are tied together?" she asked.

"I don't have proof but right now it's the straightest line of logic."

"If they were willing to kidnap me so I don't talk, then what do you think they'll do to Leslie if I share anything sensitive with you? I'm not willing to take that risk."

"You used to be one of the riskiest people I knew."

"Yeah? Well, people change."

"If I'm right and Sterling Securities is up to something illegal, then your sister's not the only one in danger. A lot of soldiers' lives are at risk."

"Fine but getting my sister back is my first priority. Agreed?"

"A hundred percent," Bronson said. "Anything you can remember will give us leverage. Right now, we've got nothing else to work with."

She walked up the steps, retrieved the hidden key behind the outdoor porch light, and inserted it into the lock, then returned to the railing. "Did you see where Mac went?"

Bronson looked around. "Probably found another animal to chase."

"Do you want to come inside?"

"I'll wait here."

"Then do ya mind to keep an eye out for Mac? I don't want to leave him behind when we head home. He's old and can't see well anymore."

"Sure. I'll hang out, make a call and be here when you're finished. We can walk back together, the three of us."

"Okay," she said and disappeared inside.

Bronson pulled his phone from his pocket and called his partner from the driveway. He didn't want Aggie to overhear his conversation.

"We need to search everything we have on Sterling Securities. I want a list of all their employees who were deployed with Aggie and everything we can find on a guy named Lee Demsky."

"Lee Demsky? Who's he?"

"Former military. Works for Sterling and according to Aggie, he's an expert drone pilot. He provides the army with surveillance of enemy targets in the field. Also, see if there's a Silverado truck registered to him or any other employee at Sterling's firm."

"Where are you? I hear a creek in the background."

Bronson looked up as Mac rounded the corner of the house, nose to the ground and headed up the front steps, taking his seat at the door.

"I'm at the Newton farm, standing outside of

Leslie's house while Aggie gets a few things. I'll probably stay here tonight just to make sure everyone's okay. I think she's in danger."

"If you say so, but I've scheduled a rotating patrol for the next few days. You really think she needs you there, too?"

Bronson trusted his partner and the Mills Creek officers. Their team, although not as large as a big city department, was experienced and had a high close rate for their cases. He'd even set up a continued training program with the nearby Charlotte Police Department to keep everyone's skills current.

He had no reason not to trust them with Aggie and her family's safety but for some reason he couldn't convince himself to go home. Old habits die hard. "I'll see how the situation feels when we get back to the main house. Did you find anything else at the scene?"

Mac stood, pawed at the door, then looked at Bronson as if he wanted to be let inside.

"We were able to collect two sets of tire tracks near the van. At least one of them was our escape vehicle."

"Let me guess. A Chevy Silverado?"

"How'd you know?"

Bronson strolled toward the porch. "They decided to pay Aggie a visit tonight. They're gone now. What about the other set of tracks?"

"A Cadillac Escalade."

"Definitely the kind of car a wealthy security owner might drive."

"And guess who leases a fleet of Cadillacs for his leadership team?"

"Palmer Sterling."

The front door clicked, and Bronson looked to see if Aggie needed help carrying anything back to the house, but she wasn't there. Mac pawed at the entrance and whined. Bronson took the steps two at a time and tried the handle. Locked.

"Why would she lock the door?"

"What?" Oz asked, still on the other end of the line.

"Let me call you back."

Bronson tapped the end key as a loud crash of glass shattered from inside. He pulled his weapon and moved to the large living room window. Scattered debris littered the floor from a broken lamp. He couldn't see much due to the darkness. Then Aggie screamed.

Her skin stung from the hit. Aggie landed on the kitchen floor and turned her cheek to the cold tile. She squeezed her eyes closed, then opened them again, righting her vision. Footsteps fell heavy behind her and she spun to face the masked intruder. Light from the large windows reflected off the barrel of his gun aimed at her head.

"Where is it?" His voice was gruff and deep, almost recognizable but she couldn't place him.

"What?"

"The USB drive. When we asked your sister about it, she said you hid it here."

"I don't know what you're talking about."

He crouched in front of her and pressed the weapon to her forehead. "Don't lie to me. Where is it?"

He wouldn't kill her. Not until he got what he wanted. She slid toward the back end of the house and rose to her feet. The island behind her displayed a collection of cast iron pans Leslie had saved after their grandmother passed away.

If Aggie was going to stay alive, then she'd have to use everything the military taught her. Some of her sparring partners were large, but this man was at least six foot three, two hundred and fifty pounds of toned muscle.

He straightened in front of her, the shape of his shoulders as wide as the bookcase behind him. "If you don't give me what I came for then we'll kill your sister."

Mac's barks grew frenzied outside the front door, and she hoped her scream alerted Bronson. Together, they could take this guy. A calm confidence washed through her, and she wrapped her fingers around the handle of a cast iron skillet before removing the pan from the hook. "You'll kill her even if I do."

"What makes you think we haven't already?" He took another step toward her, his lips curled into a snarl. "What a waste, finding out she wasn't you," he said, unaware of her newfound weapon. The darkness kept her slight movements hidden.

He was bluffing. Trying to rattle her, but she wouldn't talk no matter what he did.

Moonlight reflected off the gun pointed at her head, but instead of cowering, she straightened and braced her back foot against the cabinet. Her fingers tightened into a solid grip on the pan's handle.

"You two really do look almost identical," he continued. "But if you don't tell me where the drive is, then I'll make sure to leave some scars on your face to help distinguish you from your sister."

The front door shook as someone tried to enter. Bronson peered through the window. "Aggie? Are you okay?"

She didn't answer, returning her focus to the large man walking toward her. One more step and he'd be within reach. "I've already scared off your little friends parked in my driveway and there's no way I'm giving you anything."

He smirked. "We'll see about that."

With a quick lunge, he came at her full force. She swung. The skillet connected with the side of his head, and he staggered backward and fell to the ground. She had seconds to escape. The blow wouldn't stop him for long.

She ran to the bedroom, locked the door, and searched her sister's closet for her gun. Leslie had a concealed weapons permit and her piece had to be here somewhere. Probably high on the shelf out of Holly's reach. Her fingers fumbled across piles of T-shirts, boxes and old shoes tossed in disarray. She pulled them to the floor along with a metal box.

"There you are." Her sister's gun safe landed next to her feet, locked. Without Leslie's index fingerprint for entry, Aggie would have to find some way to pry open the lid.

She ran back into the room, searched the drawers, and found a screwdriver to use. Inside was a Glock 19. Aggie gripped the gun and lifted it from the container.

"I love you, sis."

She checked the magazine. Empty. A box of ammunition sat on a nearby shelf, as well as a pair of night vision binoculars. The head strap was missing, so she dropped them into her bag, still fastened across her body.

Her cheek ached and the vision in her left eye blurred as the swelling increased. Good thing she was right-eye dominant and could still shoot her way out.

Her fingers trembled as she pressed each bullet into the magazine, all the while trying to recall any USB drive she'd been given but nothing came to mind. All the items she'd received from the army had been returned upon discharge.

Clearly, Leslie lied, making up a location for some USB drive they wanted, but why? To keep him away from the main house? To keep him away from Holly or to lead them to Aggie so she and Bronson could arrest them?

Her attacker slammed against the door, his strength making the walls vibrate. A few more of those and the door wouldn't hold.

"If you call the cops, I'll kill your sister."

She pressed the magazine into the weapon and racked the slide to advance the first bullet into the chamber. "I thought you said you already did?"

He didn't respond. Maybe the sound of her weapon engaging would be enough to make him think twice about breaking down the door.

Aggie moved to an optimal position for her

shot. She didn't want to kill him—she needed the information he had to find her sister—but if he gave her no choice, the army taught her to never hesitate. "Tell me where she is. What have you done with Leslie?"

The sliver of light underneath the door flickered with his pacing. A strong slam shook the barrier between them again, but the door held. Her adrenaline surged, launching her mind into defense mode, military style. When the stress ramped up, her focus sharpened, and a calm moved through her body. If he entered, she was ready.

He kicked the door open. Aggie fired three rounds in succession. One grazed his shoulder, while the other two lodged into the center mass of a Kevlar vest. He retreated into the kitchen.

She shot two more times before Bronson busted into the room with Mac at his heels.

Her attacker took one look at the dog, ran out the back door and disappeared outside.

Bronson motioned for her to follow. "I'll go around, cut him off."

The cold night air stung Aggie's injury and her left eye watered, but she kept moving. Droplets of blood dotted the deck boards providing a trail to follow with caution. Her father always said a wounded animal was the most unpredictable and dangerous when cornered and bound to attack. But she couldn't let this man run off to lick his wounds. Not when he was the best lead she had to find Leslie. She closed her eyes, inhaled, and listened.

The creek to her left rushed.

Tree frogs chirped.

A branch snapped to her right.

Her eyes opened and Aggie pivoted her aim. The man ran across the yard toward the trees. She fired two more rounds but missed and took off after him into the woods.

Short bursts of her breath misted the air as she reached the tree line. Movement near Leslie's back shed caught her attention. Bronson stood at the corner and signaled to a large rock off the beaten path, then he disappeared from sight at the other end of the wooded area.

She entered the thick brush, keeping her steps light and headed toward the rock near an old service road that ran along the back of Leslie's property. Probably the intruder's alternate escape route.

The overgrowth of mountain laurels, azalea buds and saplings complicated her trek. Briars snagged her jeans and tore at her skin—the area hadn't been cleared since they were kids. Ignoring the pain, she kept moving.

Her father, who loved hunting outdoors, had taught her to scan the ground for tracks and disturbed soil while checking for broken branches on outstretched limbs. A man the size of her intruder couldn't come through here without disturbing the natural environment and leaving a few shoe prints in the soft soil.

She scanned the ground.

A gunshot split the air.

Bronson.

All thoughts of stealth forgotten, Aggie took off running toward the sound.

Please God. Don't let him be hurt.

Voices echoed through the air. They sounded frantic. She drew closer, slowing her steps and taking cover behind a tree. A strong hand gripped her shoulder. Aggie froze.

FOUR

Bronson exhaled with relief when Aggie faced him. "I thought they shot you."

She raised her face to the dim moonlight. Massive bruises covered her jaw, and her eye was swollen. Rage rose through every fiber of his body.

"He did this to you?" Bronson reached out and gently touched her cheek.

She pulled his hand away. "This is nothing. I've learned how to take a beating over the years. Did you find him?"

He motioned to the top of the embankment. "He's headed to the service road and his cronies are waiting for him. That's their escape."

"We have to stop them."

"I've called for backup but there's a large car wreck in the middle of town blocking traffic and they're at least twenty minutes out, except for the patrol officer I asked Oz to station at the main house, but I'd rather leave him in place."

"Absolutely. I want Mom and Holly to have extra protection. You and I can find them."

"How much ammo do you have left?"

Aggie released the gun's magazine. "Ten rounds plus one in the chamber, but if we're going to find Leslie then we need at least one of them alive."

"I'm hoping we have them all arrested by the end of the night."

She reached into her bag and handed Bronson the night vision goggles. "These might help."

The gray truck sat on the service road at the bottom of the embankment, idling with headlights shining. To their right, the intruder lumbered down the embankment toward the vehicle. Blood dripped from the man's fingers and stained his arm.

Bronson lowered the goggles. "Did you shoot him?"

"I think I hit his shoulder. Probably a surface wound because he barely slowed after the shot."

"I don't know. He's cradling that arm pretty tight across his chest. Tells me you did a bit more damage than a flesh wound."

"Let me see?"

He handed the goggles back to her.

"By the way, where's Mac?" she asked while adjusting the focus dial.

"I left him in the fenced back yard. I didn't think you'd want him near any gunfire."

"Thanks. I'm glad he's safe. Make a mental note that my attacker doesn't like dogs. He took one look at Mac and made a beeline for the exit."

"That dog heard the commotion first and started pawing at the door but by the time I got through you'd already shot the guy." He pointed toward the road. "Looks like there's at least two others inside the cab. The incline must be steep since our boy hasn't joined them yet."

"You think we can catch him before he gets in the truck?"

"Doubtful."

She wiped the lens with the bottom of her shirt. "My dad and I used to walk this road all the time. We can cut them off farther down if we hurry. If they get to the interstate, they'll escape."

"What's your plan?"

"There's a narrow trail along the edge of this rock face that can take us around, but we have to pass right over them. As long as we don't shift any loose rocks their way, they won't even look up to see us on the trail."

"And how do we get to the other side of this boulder mound? It's at least eight feet tall."

Aggie hiked her foot off the ground. "Boost me up, will ya?"

"I guess that means we're walking the narrow ledge that drops straight down at least three hundred feet? The one your mother always told us to stay away from when we were kids?"

"Yeah. Is that a problem?"

"Maybe not for your ballerina feet, but my big clunkers are likely to slip."

"Fine. Stay here and I'll go."

"I'm not letting you go alone. It's just that—"

"Please don't tell me you're afraid of heights."

That's exactly what he was going to say but changed his mind when he saw the look on her moonlit face. She placed a hand on his shoulder. "If I can jump out of helicopters at thirty thousand feet, you can do this. Just don't look down."

"Yeah, people always say that." Bronson extended his hand and a knee for her to use as a stepping stool. "And of course, it makes everyone look down right before they plummet to their death."

She belly-crawled over the ledge and leaned back over. "What was that?"

"Nothing."

She extended a hand for his. "All clear. Let's go, Molasses."

"Cute." He slapped his hand into hers and

muscled his way over the boulder as well. Even though he dreaded to walk the narrow ledge, her idea was their best option and once Aggie had an idea in her head, there was no backing down. He imagined she was a force to be reckoned with when she was in the army.

Bronson kept low and followed her, leaning into the rock. He prayed God wouldn't let him slip.

Aggie made a hand signal indicating the truck was right below them. He tried not to look down, but the urge was too great. His upper body weaved a bit as he took in the height of their position, and he placed one hand on the rock face to steady his gait. His insides tightened with nausea. With a deep breath in, he placed one foot in front of the other, careful not to knock any gravel over the ledge.

A break in the trees gave way to brighter moonlight and exposed their position all the way to the road, but their attackers never looked up.

Bronson rushed his last few steps and strength returned to his legs with the wider path. He joined Aggie as she crouched low and watched the men through her binoculars.

"The guy who attacked me just made it to the truck and they're dressing his wound. We don't have much time and need to move if we're going to get ahead of them to block the road."

"Can you see the driver's face?"

She handed the binoculars to him. One man, standing outside the driver's side door, was almost as tall as Aggie's attacker, but even with night vision goggles, his image was too grainy from this distance. The intruder pulled off his mask but kept his back to the woods. Bronson scanned to the bed of the truck.

"You ready?" Aggie said.

"Not quite. They've got several semiautomatic weapons near the tailgate and two other men with them. Let me find out the ETA of our backup units. We're going to need help blocking the exit at the main road with that kind of fire power. Hopefully, they're close by now."

Bronson connected with dispatch. The other officers were five minutes out and wouldn't arrive in time unless he slowed the suspects down. "Didn't there used to be a gate across this road to keep trespassers from hunting without permission?"

"Yeah. It's about five hundred yards that way, around a curve and down a slight hill."

Bronson took one more look at the men. They'd never stop hunting Aggie, and this might be his only chance to grab at least one of them. He straightened. "Let's go."

"What are we doing?"

"My team's five minutes out and we need to stall. If we lock the gate across the road then that will slow them down until the other officers arrive."

He headed down the hill with Aggie following close behind.

"They didn't look like they were in any hurry to leave," she said. "Maybe they're planning to hit the house again."

"Why would they do that?"

"The guy who attacked me mentioned a USB drive."

"You never mentioned a drive to me."

"Because I don't know what he's talking about. He said my sister told him it was in the house. You don't think he'll go to the main house..."

She stopped walking. "What if Mom and Holly are in trouble? I should go back."

"Your mom and Holly are safe. Oz stationed a patrol officer right outside their door, remember? They won't go back." Bronson kept walking. "Did he say what was on the drive?"

"No, just that Leslie told him I'd hidden it there, but I returned all of my equipment into the army upon discharge. I brought my personal laptop home, but there's nothing tied to the government on it."

He increased his pace to a jog, weaving in and out of thickets and thorns. "Did you check all your belongings? Maybe you missed something. You get to keep some of your clothing and army bags, right?"

The path widened and Aggie ran beside him. "Yeah, the stuff I purchased with my own money, but I haven't had a chance to go through anything yet. I've got one of my flight suits and bag that I brought home."

"And you don't have any idea what might be on this drive?"

"No clue. The government doesn't let us use them so the information can't be tied to any of my missions. Our laptops don't give us the option to export anything to external devices. One of the many ways they keep everything secure."

"What if someone was keeping a personal record of government interactions and saved their own note files to a drive? Then, they could sell that information to the highest bidder, correct?"

"True, but that still doesn't answer why they think *I* have a USB with anything like that on it. I certainly didn't keep any personal record about our missions."

"Doesn't mean someone less loyal didn't do exactly that. Especially if they worked for Sterling. They have employees stationed on all the bases who provide surveillance, guard duty and tactical support when needed. They could've kept notes or stolen files without the government knowing, especially with the high-level cybersecurity experts they employ. With Palmer talking to you at the diner, an employee like Lee could be our connection."

She kept up her pace beside him and jogged for a moment in silence. "I've had a few operations that didn't go as planned, but nearly all the missions assigned to my flight book were carried out without any issues."

"Was Corbin killed in one of the operations that went wrong?"

Her jog slowed to a walk, and she pointed down the hill, avoiding his question. "There's the gate."

Bronson descended the steep embankment with Aggie right behind him. With a jerk of the latch, he freed the bar to swing across.

Aggie pulled the other arm of the gate towards the middle of the road, and he threaded the chain through the lock to secure the gate in place. They returned to the side of the road and hid in the thick underbrush.

"I already know he was part of a mission to extract an interpreter and his family from Afghanistan," Bronson said. "I also know Corbin was shot during the mission."

"Where did you hear that?"

"I called in a few favors and requested documents through the Department of Defense. Most of the report was redacted but I was able to put a few things together."

She let out a sigh and then seemed to come to terms with opening up a little more. "The unit came under heavy fire that night."

"And my brother?"

"According to the reports, everything turned to chaos after the units were dropped into their location, but he completed his mission and helped the team escape."

Bronson's heart rate quickened. "Did the report name the team members? Maybe I could talk to someone who was with him."

She straightened and moved further into the cover of the trees, standing behind a large oak with a diameter to shield them both. "I can't say more than I already have. And some of the answers you want, I honestly don't know."

This was the first time she'd slightly opened up to him. After almost a year, the puzzle of his brother's death had a few more pieces, but he wanted the whole picture. He'd never have closure without knowing, but now was not the time to push.

A glow of blue lights flickered in the darkness several yards away. "Backup's here."

He nodded in their direction and radioed his

partner. "Cut your lights. Leave the spike strips and cars blocking the exit but move the officers toward the position of the gate. Remain out of sight until I give the signal."

"Ten-four," Oz responded.

The flash disappeared and Bronson faced Aggie, who stood with her right shoulder leaned against the tree.

"I hope this works," she said.

He stepped closer to her in order to keep his body concealed from the road. "It will. They've got nowhere else to go. Officers are positioned on both sides. When the truck gets to the gate, they'll rush in and take these guys into custody. Once they're processed, we'll interrogate them until they tell us where Leslie's located. She'll be home before the sun comes up."

Aggie's hand touched his arm, stirring feelings he'd chosen to ignore since her return.

"Thank you for helping me. I knew I could count on you." Her gaze lifted to his. She didn't move her hand but instead slid it to his chest.

Their first kiss had been in the woods after a day of hiking. He'd pulled her off the trail and into the shadows of the trees to make sure no one saw his public display of affection. He even told his mom when he returned home that she was the one. Funny how things changed.

He leaned his body back, giving himself a bit more space. "It's my job."

Ending his relationship with her was the hardest decision he'd made, but his choice had been the right one. The secrets between them had created too much of a wedge to overcome.

She let her hand fall and peeked back around the tree. "What if they realize this is an ambush and bail instead of getting out to open the gate?"

"My officers are well trained. They'll move in and take the suspects into custody while they're still scratching their heads trying to figure out what happened."

"I just have a bad feeling. You know? That sinking ache deep inside right before everything goes up in smoke." Stress etched lines into her forehead and she leaned closer to him. "Do you think this will trigger them to hurt Leslie?"

He fought the urge to pull her into his arms and make promises he wasn't sure he could keep. "I'm doing everything in my power to get her back, safe and sound."

"I know," she said, her voice soft.

Her quiet demeanor lured him closer—the scent of her muted perfume, the strand of dark hair framing her face, the closeness of her body—all weakened his resolve. Aggie leaned in, brushing her lips against his.

He didn't respond and tried to ignore the tingle of her peppermint chapstick sending shivers from his lips through the rest of his body. He'd not kissed anyone since her, but the pain of loss rose above the desire to kiss her back.

Bronson shook his head. "Don't."

Her fingers covered her mouth and tears pooled in her eyes. "I've missed you."

"We can't do this again," he said.

"But—"

"That chapter of our lives is over. We've both moved on."

"Have we?"

The question caught him off guard. They'd been apart for a year. He'd been out with a couple of women since her but none of them even came close to the natural connection they had. "If we're going to work together then we have to have some boundaries."

She stepped back and eyed him for a moment longer. "I wasn't trying to make you uncomfortable."

"You didn't."

"I see. Then I guess one of us *has* moved on."

He'd ended their relationship and needed to be strong now or they'd wind up right back where they were a year ago—heartbroken.

He couldn't go through losing her again. Not a second time. "I can't go back."

"Can't or won't?"

He ignored her question and lifted the night vision goggles from her hand. "Let's just focus on the operation."

Aggie placed her back against the tree and swiped the tears from her cheeks. She wasn't the kind of woman who cried easily, and he hated the thought that he'd hurt her—but he needed to focus on the task at hand and keep his guard up. If he started focusing on what she was feeling instead of the danger they were facing, the chances went way up of someone getting hurt. No one should discuss relationship issues on three cups of coffee and late-night hours anyway unless they wanted a foolish outcome.

Headlights flickered around the bend. Bronson clicked his radio and lowered his voice. "Target's in motion."

The gray truck rounded the curve, then slowed several feet from the gate. The headlights brightened.

Bronson scanned the road. "Come on," he whispered. "Get out of the truck."

He radioed Oz. "Hold your positions. I want them away from the guns in the back. They have to get out to unlock the gate, then we'll move in."

Seconds seemed to tick by in hours and Bronson's heartbeat pulsed heavy through him. No one got out of the vehicle. Instead, the truck reversed course, turned in the middle of the road and raced back up the mountain.

"All units move in. Suspects are headed north on SR273."

He and Aggie ran down the hill and opened the gate, while officers hurried to their cars.

"They're getting away," she said.

Bronson grabbed the chain and unhooked the ends. Aggie pulled her side open to unblock the road. Two police cars flew by them, chasing their suspects, sirens and lights in full display.

Oz was in an unmarked SUV and stopped when he reached them. "Get in."

They jumped inside.

"Is there another way out?" Oz asked, glancing in the rearview mirror at Aggie.

"The road is only two miles long. I thought there was a dead end at the top, but why would they run that way if they weren't sure there was an exit?"

Bronson enlarged the GPS map on Oz's police computer. "Looks like there's been an extension added. The road exits onto the Blue Ridge Parkway. If we don't stop them, they'll escape. Again."

Oz pressed the gas and flew around mountainous switchback curves, each one steeper than the next. "Seems like this road flattens out at the top."

With a click of his radio, Bronson contacted the lead cruiser. "Officer 321-Charley, have y'all got sights on the truck?"

"Negative. We split up on the parkway. I went north. No sightings yet."

They reached the top and Oz stopped at the end of road. "Which way? One of the two lead cars should have a visual by now. The road is two lanes all the way to Henderson."

"Where'd they go?" Bronson looked to his right. Then to the left. A large overlook sat straight across from them with no boundary to the death-defying drop below.

Something moved in his side mirror, then a hard hit slammed them from the rear. Oz hit the brakes and the scent of burning rubber filled the SUV as the gray truck pushed them forward. Bronson gripped the dashboard. "Oz. Get us out of here. Do something."

"I'm trying but they've got more power."

The truck let off for a moment, then rammed them again, shoving their vehicle toward the steep mountainous descent.

Aggie's head jolted forward, only her seat belt keeping her body from slamming into the driver's seat. She turned and looked out the back window. "How'd they get behind us?"

"No idea," Oz said, glancing into the rearview again. He hit the gas and steered the car sideways into the overlook, keeping them from barreling over the edge of the mountain.

"They must've pulled off into the bushes at the flat area half a mile back," Bronson said. "Here they come again."

Oz maneuvered out of the way, his tires spinning on the asphalt. Aggie clung to the handle above her head and prayed for protection. At this rate, she'd have whiplash for sure, even if she survived the onslaught of attacks. Their vehicle fishtailed. Oz regained control and punched the gas pedal, jolting them forward so hard the force pinned Aggie to her seat.

"We need to get behind them," Bronson said.

Oz's attempts to outrun the truck were futile. Bright lights blinded Aggie's vision. Tires squealed and metal crunched against the back fender.

With another hit, their SUV sailed into the air over the side of the mountain.

Weightless and dropping, Aggie's arms flailed, fumbling for anything to grasp. She found the door handle and anchored her body as best she could. Even belted, she flipped upside down with the roll of the SUV. Glass shattered and peppered her with shards. Cold air whooshed against her skin. With the blunt impact, her body swung into the air bag as the car came to a rest on its passenger side.

Pain pierced her head. She opened her eyes and tried to regain her bearings. The vehicle rocked and tilted toward the rear.

Bronson didn't look back but remained stoic in the passenger seat. "Are y'all okay?"

"A little rattled and bruised, maybe with a few scrapes from broken glass, but I don't think I'm seriously hurt," Aggie said, with Oz adding his agreement.

"I think I'm good too," Bronson said, his gaze snapping toward her when she reached for her buckle.

He held up his hand. "Don't. We need to maintain the balance in the vehicle. If you unbuckle, then we could tip. I'm not sure how long the trees will hold us. Stay still."

She followed his instructions, surprised at the look of sheer panic on his face. Bronson always carried himself with confidence. His wide eyes and death grip on the door handle right now proved just how deep his fear of heights really went.

Oz radioed for help. "Officer 287-Adam. We've got a 10-54 with two officers and one civilian in need of assistance with an extraction. The drop is steep so use caution. All other units—BOLO for a gray, late model Chevrolet Silverado 3500 Series. Vehicle headed southbound on the Blue Ridge Parkway."

The caller came back. "How steep of a drop?"

"Three hundred feet, almost straight down."

"We'll have to call in Fire and Rescue. They're equipped with rappel equipment. Sit tight. It'll take them at least thirty minutes to get there."

The radio fell silent and Aggie pulled her phone from her back pants pocket, then turned on the flashlight. Bronson was right. The only thing between them and the black abyss below was a couple of trees. She looked back up the mountain and several of the officers involved in the chase parked their cars at the top with their blue lights flashing. The extraction team would have no problem finding their location, but every time the wind blew, the SUV creaked and triggered another desperate prayer of protection from her silent lips to God.

Bronson turned on his flashlight, too. "We've got to get out of here."

"Just sit still," Oz said, keeping his hands on the steering wheel. "If we move too much, then this vehicle could teeter off the trees. You don't want that, do you?"

The prominence of Bronson's Adam's apple

bobbed with a swallow. "Of course not, but we can't sit here and wait for thirty minutes."

"Yes, we can," Aggie said. "We don't really have any other choice." She looked out the opposite rear window. Darkness cloaked the drop below and fear of the unknown filled every part of her body. She was used to being able to distinguish the ground from the sky above, but at the moment, there was nothing but a black velvet void.

"Maybe we could sing a song or something," Oz suggested. "Take our minds—"

"No." Both of them responded at the same time.

"Fine. I'll turn on the radio."

Country tunes filtered through the speakers and Aggie did feel herself relax a little. "Thanks, Oz. That's better."

"Yeah, kind of like the string quartet that played while the *Titanic* sank," Bronson said.

No sooner had the words left his mouth when another gust of wind blew against them, even stronger than before. The vehicle rocked backward. Bronson's grip on his seat belt tightened and Aggie closed her eyes, waiting on the weightless feeling of falling to start again.

The movement settled and Aggie released the breath she'd been holding.

"Call them back. See if they're here yet."

Bronson white-knuckled the door grip and kept his eyes closed when he made the request.

Oz tilted his wrist to view his watch. "It's only been ten minutes."

"I don't care. Call them." Bronson's words were clipped with anxiety.

His partner clicked the radio again. "Officer 287-Adam to dispatch. Requesting update please."

Static filtered through. "ETA two minutes. Ahead of schedule. Give them time to gear up and we'll have y'all out in a few minutes."

Red lights from the rescue truck added another swirl of color above Aggie's head. Within the next ten minutes, bright head lamps descended toward them and glared into her eyes. A young man outfitted with ropes corded across his body and extra harnesses clipped to his belt tapped on Oz's driver's side window.

"Y'all need a lift?"

"Cute," Bronson said. "Just get us out of here."

"Any injuries I'm working with?"

Oz shook his head. "Nothing more than a few scratches and bruises."

"Great. We're waiting on the team above to provide our lighting, then we'll secure the front of the car with a strap and drive security hooks into the rock."

A hum buzzed overhead, and a bright floodlight switched on from above. Oz leaned forward and looked out through the windshield. "Is that a drone?"

"Yeah." The guy smiled. "One of our latest toys. Darkness is the most challenging part of a mountain rescue so when Sterling Securities offered to let us test these out, we accepted."

The drone lit up the entire area, clarifying their position. A large rock outcropping was a hundred feet below them before dropping off still farther into a turbulent river.

The young guy moved to Aggie and her broken back window. "Let's start with you first. Since the car is unstable in the rear, removing the extra weight will make the front more secure."

"You sure know how to sweet talk a lady, don't ya?"

In the glare of the flood light, she could see the guy blush as he stammered to reply. "I didn't mean you were fat... I just meant—"

Aggie held up her hand. "Don't worry. I'm just teasing. Something I do when I'm nervous. Anyway, what do you want me to do?"

He handed her a harness to slip her legs through and clipped a tandem rope to the carabiner. He tightened the support and reached for her hand after she unbuckled her seat belt.

"Nice and slow. We're going to ease you out through the window."

"Were you able to secure the car?" she asked.

"Not completely, but it's better than before. The drop's too steep at the back to attach a hold. Keep your movements minimal."

She placed a hand on her cross-body bag, the zipped-up contents still secure, then reached for his grip with trembling fingers. This wasn't the time to let fear reign.

He clipped an extra rope to her that fastened around his body. "Ready?"

"As I'll ever be."

With an affirmative command, he pulled her from the backseat, lifting her from the car in one fell swoop. She looked back and watched as the car reflector lights swayed a little before settling. Oz and Bronson were still inside the vehicle with another rescuer helping Oz into his harness.

They hung above the scene about twenty feet, when their ascent slowed. Her rescuer released her waist, moving back a little to show her what to do. "Since this is a steep climb, you want to sit back in the harness and keep your feet out in front of you. The winch will pull us up the rest of the way and the boys will help at the top. Okay?"

"Got it. Thanks."

The process was slow, but Aggie finally reached flat footing at the top of the ridge. She turned back to watch the others. Oz started his climb with only Bronson left in the SUV. Metal creaked and scraped across the bark a few inches. The vehicle shifted and angled a bit as he moved into the driver's seat. They handed him a harness.

"Can't you move faster to get him out of there?" she asked, still wearing her harness, rope attached.

He wound his rope in a figure eight pattern over his arm and slid it back into the labeled compartment. "We're going as fast as we can. Move too quick and we could send him on down the mountain."

"But the strap on the SUV will hold, right?"

"Should."

Not the confident answer she wanted. She prayed God would protect Bronson. They might not be a couple anymore, but she still had feelings for him. All those years they'd been together, she'd thought she'd found her person for the rest of her life. Even after a year, it was sometimes hard to convince herself that their relationship was really over.

Everyone told her long-distance deployments were challenging, but she'd seen hundreds of couples survive the demands of the military. When Bronson moved to Fayetteville, she thought they were strong enough to handle several months at a time with her overseas. And they had, until Corbin was killed. Then everything changed.

"What's taking so long?" Looking around, she realized there was no one within earshot to answer. She refocused on Bronson. Shadowed movements inside the SUV gave way to a view of his face. He gripped the rim of the driver's side window and reached for the officer's safety rope to clip to his harness.

They never connected.

With a sudden snap, the strap on the vehicle broke and sent the SUV backward into a dark abyss. Bronson disappeared over the side of the ledge.

FIVE

Bronson had just grabbed the sides of the window to pull himself out when he felt the car shift. He launched his body from the vehicle but missed the rescuer's hand, landing against the steep embankment and tumbling for what seemed an eternity. Every roll added another cut or bruise to his body, ending with a slam against a large tree anchored to the last narrow ledge before plunging into the raging river underneath.

A sharp pain shot up his side and he struggled to breathe. He wiggled his fingers and toes to make sure there were no spinal injuries and assessed his legs and arms for any breaks.

With a sigh of relief, he realized that other than a few minor scrapes, some contusions and probably a couple broken ribs, he was okay. He'd survived. He pressed up, placed his back against the trunk and thanked God he was alive.

Commands, shouts, and the clip of carabiners echoed from above. Officers, determined to reach him, descended on their ropes and triggered showers of loose rock and debris. He waited, still struggling to breathe, and prayed the climb back up wouldn't be too painful.

Light footsteps thumped next to him on the narrow ledge.

"Bronson? Thank goodness. You're alive." Aggie knelt and took his hand.

"How'd you get down so quick?" he asked, surprised she'd made the descent faster than the other rescuers.

"I'm a soldier, remember? Rappelling is like breathing, especially for a helicopter pilot. We practiced often."

He laughed, then grabbed his ribs. "I think I'm going to have trouble breathing for a while."

She lifted his arm and tucked her small frame under his shoulder. He flinched with pain. "Easy. That's the side that hurts."

After a quick apology, she moved to his other side and helped him to his feet. "The other officers were grabbing harnesses and extra ropes to get you back to the top. They should be here soon."

"And Oz? How's he?"

"Made it to the top, just as you dropped."

Bronson tried to take a step and doubled over in pain.

"Stay still. You need a hospital and an x-ray of your ribs."

"I'll be fine. Just need some sleep, that's all. Not like much is done for broken ribs anyway. They don't even recommend taping or wrapping them anymore because it restricts deep breathing and contributes to pneumonia."

"Still won't hurt to have an emergency room doc take a look at ya, just to make sure."

"A buddy of mine cracked a rib a few months back, but the hospital sent him home with little more than some ibuprofen and one heck of a bill. I'll pass."

More debris sprinkled from above and reflectors sewn into the rescuers' uniforms caught the light halfway down the embankment.

"They're almost here," she said.

"What about our attackers? Did anyone find the truck?"

"Not yet, as far as I know."

An awkward silence stretched between them.

She stepped a little closer and lowered her voice. "Look. About earlier when we were in the woods. I shouldn't have kiss—"

"We can just let it go." He waved a hand and disrupted the insects swarming in the bright light.

"You were right. We need to stay clearheaded to find my sister. I apologize for letting the moment cloud my judgment."

"No need to apologize. Maybe we consider that a goodbye kiss and move forward as friends."

"Do you really think exes can be friends?"

He shrugged, then flinched when the movement jarred his ribs. "You've got a point. How about professional colleagues. After we find your sister, we can go our separate ways."

She looked back up the mountain. "If that's what you want."

A bit of dust and gravel sprinkled over them, as two rescuers touched down. He didn't get to ask her what she wanted but it might be best if he didn't know.

Aggie stepped forward and helped the officer with the extra harness and ropes. They worked as a team to secure Bronson in place without causing him more pain. When they were ready, officers at the top of the embankment activated the winch. Bronson breathed through the stabbing pain in his chest, reminding himself that it was temporary. Maybe one day the pain of losing Aggie would pass, too.

He made the climb to level ground and the paramedic assessed his injuries, finding mostly bruising and abrasions.

"We can't be sure without an x-ray if your ribs are fractured, but from what you've described and the location of your pain, that's probably the case. As long as you're breathing okay, your lungs are in good shape. When the ambulance gets here, we can take you to the emergency room and get an official diagnosis."

"I'm not going to the hospital," Bronson said.

The paramedic shot him a look. "You need to get checked out."

"They can't do anything for broken ribs anyway. I'm able to breathe and I've got a kidnapped woman to find."

"I'm going to document in my notes that you're refusing to come with us to the emergency room. I can't make you, but I think you're making a mistake."

"I promise if the pain gets worse in the next few days, I'll see my regular doctor."

"Suit yourself." The man opened the cabinet, pulled out a chemical cold pack and activated it with his hands. "Keep this or ice on it for the next twenty-four to forty-eight hours to help with inflammation. I can give you some pain meds if you want, or you can take ibuprofen and acetaminophen over the counter. Your choice."

"I'll stick with over-the-counter pain meds."

"The fractures should heal on their own

within six to eight weeks, but the severe pain should subside in a few days. Even if you do improve, it might not be a bad idea to call your doctor and tell him about the accident. Then, he can follow up and make sure you don't have any lingering issues from the trauma."

Gravel crunched behind him as he placed the cold compress to his side. Aggie had reached the top of the parkway overlook and removed her harness and ropes before joining him. "Ready to go the hospital?"

"Like I said, there's not much they can do for me there. I think I'll head home instead."

She folded her arms across her chest. "Then you're coming home with me. We have a guest room, and I can take you to the emergency department if it turns out your injuries are worse than you realize."

"Thanks for the offer but really I'll be fine at my own place."

"I won't take no for an answer." Aggie turned to Oz. "We're taking him to my house. Do you care to ask one of your officers to drive us?"

Oz twirled his key ring around his index finger and looked at Bronson. "Sounds good to me."

"Really? You're taking her side?"

His partner gave him a little salute and walked off to arrange their ride as Bronson's phone vibrated in his pocket. The text was from his sergeant, but the message wasn't good news.

The intruders escaped
They'll come for Aggie
Increasing her security detail

He pressed the lock button on his phone. "Actually, Aggie. You're right. I probably shouldn't be alone. If we could swing by my place first so I can pack a bag that would be great. Then we can go to your house."

"Wow. I'm stunned, but glad you see the logic in staying at the farm."

He smiled and slid his cell back into his pocket. If the criminals who wanted Aggie were still out there, then he wasn't taking any chances with her safety, and that meant sticking close whether he wanted to or not.

Aggie opened the door to her family's guest room and dropped Bronson's duffel bag by the queen bed. Her mother kept the room spotless in case a weary traveler or family member needed a reprieve for the night. She was glad for her mother's preparedness—it saved them time now. It was almost three o'clock in the morning and her body longed for her comfy mattress, but slumber would have to wait a bit longer until she had Bronson settled.

She folded down the white duvet cover and gray sheets on the bed. Fresh flowers filled a vase on the nightstand, next to two bottled waters. Her mother must've dressed the room after she texted to let her know they'd have a guest. Aggie had hated to wake her up in the middle of the night, but better that than Bronson getting shot because her mother thought there was an intruder.

Hardwood floors creaked underneath her feet when she walked to the window and closed the dark blue curtains.

"Shower's in here." She flipped on the light in the adjoining bathroom and glanced over her shoulder at him. "And you need one."

"Really?" He sniffed his shirt. "You don't like the outdoorsy type?"

"Not when the smell is mixed with polecat and mountain mud." She scrunched her nose. "There's towels and soap in there and the shampoo's in the linen closet. Mom keeps the good stuff in the back."

He ran a hand over the dark stubble lining his jawline. "How about a razor?"

"Middle shelf."

"Your mom really does think of everything. Did you tell her I was coming?"

"She always keeps the guest room stocked for unexpected guests—and yes, I texted her to let her know you'd be staying a few days but try not to scare her by making too much noise. She keeps a shotgun by her bed."

"Sounds like all of the Newton women are sharpshooters."

"We have our moments. And don't tell her about what happened to us tonight. She's got enough to worry about with Leslie, and I don't want to add to that. I'll leave a note letting her know we made it in safely on the kitchen counter, so she'll see it when she gets up." Aggie glanced at her watch. "I know it's late but if you're hungry, there's a plate of cookies with a pitcher of tea in the fridge. Do you want me to bring you up anything before I go to bed?"

"I'm pretty beat. I'll try the cookies tomorrow."

Leaf fragments stuck in his sandy brown hair and a smudge of dirt dotted his cheek right below his clear blue eyes. No one should look so handsome while covered in debris. She had to get away from him or her heart might never recover. The sooner they found Leslie, the sooner she could get on with her life and find someone new. Someone without all the baggage piled up between them.

Aggie crossed the room, tipped up on her

toes in front of him and tried to pull a leaf from his hair. He stepped back and she missed.

"What are you doing?" he asked.

"Hold still."

This time Bronson didn't move, and she snatched the leaf. A faint hint of spiced cologne still lingered on his T-shirt. The same kind he wore when they dated. "Remember when you thought it would be fun to take me mudding in an ATV?"

"How could I forget? We went to Old Man Kennerly's place. There had been a deluge the night before and the puddles were extra full. We came back to your house covered from head to toe. Your mom sprayed us down in the yard with the garden hose."

She sniffed his shirt. "I think you smell worse tonight."

Bronson flashed his knee-weakening smile and she held out the leaf for him to take, but he folded his hand over hers. "I think you should keep it. Something to remember me by when this is all over."

"Not like we won't see each other again," she said. "I'm staying for good this time. My military career is over, and my family needs me. I'm sure we'll bump into each other around town."

"I guess there's something I need to tell you then." He moved his hand from hers. "After I close this case, I'm taking a job down in Charlotte. A friend of mine is the captain there. He convinced me to take a sergeant position and run his homicide division."

His revelation stunned her. Deep down, she'd hoped to bridge the gap between her and Bronson now that she was back. But they needed to be in the same town if she had any chance of rebuilding their relationship.

"Oh. I didn't know."

"Mills Creek is my hometown, but I miss the activity of a large department."

"Not enough action here for you?"

"Not like Charlotte."

"Of course. Congratulations, then." She moved toward the door, paused, and turned back to face him. Her training in the military had taught her to guard her emotions, to never show weakness, but if he was leaving Mills Creek, then she had nothing to lose by being honest.

"I don't need a leaf to remember you by, Bronson. There's no way I could forget you. I'm just sorry we weren't able to make things work because I would've liked that."

She closed the door before he responded, unable to handle any more of his rejection.

Not again.

Not this time.

Not with Leslie missing.

* * *

As Aggie walked back to her bedroom, each creak of the hallway floor brought back memories of her father. He'd been married to her mom for forty years before he passed. They had an everlasting love, secured by their faith in God. Not that they didn't have issues, but they always worked things out. If she didn't figure out a way to get over Bronson, she might never find a Godly man to share her life and end up alone.

Aggie continued up the steps to the second-floor landing and moved as quietly as she could. She didn't want to wake her mom and niece, just like her father tried to keep from waking her when she was little. The weight and pace of his steps echoed in her mind. Sometimes he'd peek his head into her room to say goodnight and if she managed to still be awake, she would weasel a second bedtime story out of him.

Her fingertips traced the faded pink heart sticker with her name on the door of her bedroom. Leslie had one, too, but hers was purple on the third door at the end of the hall—the room where Holly was sleeping tonight.

Aggie entered, her army flight bag sat in the corner chair, and she unzipped the opening. Exhaustion permeated every ounce of her body, but if she didn't at least look for the mentioned USB, then she'd never get any sleep.

With a shake of the bag, she dumped all of the contents onto the floor. Dirty clothes, personal items, and various tokens she brought back from Afghanistan covered the area, but there was no USB drive. She sorted through the contents carefully. Maybe something in the pile would provide a clue to why someone targeted her and her family.

A small photo book stuck out from one of the interior pockets. She pulled it from the slot and leaned back against her pillows. During her loneliest moments, these mementos from home had kept her from descending into tears.

She flipped through each picture, taking the time to recall the events. Most were photos of friends and family, including a few of her sister from when they were younger. With a turn to the back, she stopped. The obituary her mother sent from their hometown paper filled the slot. She unfolded the piece and looked at the picture. Corbin's infectious smile stared back at her. He'd died way too young, and she couldn't help feeling that his death was all her fault.

She'd flown hundreds of missions with minimal incidents, dropping off troops in dangerous terrain or urban cities teeming with hostile combatants. She'd dodged rockets and gunfire, always doing her utmost to deliver her troops to safety.

She nearly always succeeded. Nearly.

But his last mission had been a horror show that still weighed on her.

Corbin had advanced to sergeant and had a reputation for great leadership ability. Watching him that night, she could tell that he'd earned the respect of his soldiers. Not every sergeant she'd encountered met that same level of acceptance and trust. His death had been a loss, not only for the army, but for her and his family.

She read down the page where they gave him full military honors at his burial. Only twenty-four years old.

Perhaps, if she'd maneuvered the chopper to a different location, he might still be alive. One shot. Right through the anterior portion of his shoulder, piercing his subclavian artery. Their medic had tried to save him, but his wound was fatal.

She closed the book and stared at the ceiling fan rotating counterclockwise. Something had changed in her that night. Something that had turned her dream job into a nightmare, eventually leading her to leave the army altogether.

The desperate look in Bronson's eyes whenever he talked about Corbin pierced her heart even more. How could she ever forgive herself for not protecting his brother?

Aggie wiped the wetness from her cheeks and put the photos away. If she didn't find this drive, then her sister would end up like Corbin and she would never recover.

She searched every pocket of her bag again. Empty. This was her only piece of luggage and the small amount of furniture she owned was scheduled to arrive next week but with her sister's disappearance, she planned to push that out until after they were all together again.

Aggie sifted through all her clothes a second time. Mounds of T-shirts, pants, shorts and even one dress held nothing but leftover sand from the Afghan desert.

With a turn in the middle of the room, she scanned the floor. The sleeve of her flight suit stuck out from under the bed—and at the sight of it, she suddenly remembered. She dropped to her knees, patted the pockets, and hit something small and hard.

"There you are."

Aggie retrieved the USB and held the device between her fingers. After Corbin was shot, she went back to her chopper. There, underneath one of the passenger seats, she'd found the drive and tucked it into her pocket for safekeeping. She had planned to turn it in, but with Corbin's death consuming her thoughts, the USB vanished from her mind until now.

She scanned the mess for her laptop, ready to find out what was on the drive. Maybe the files would give them the information they needed to find Leslie. But before she could excavate her computer, a soft knock rapped against her door, interrupting her plan.

Aggie shoved the drive under her pillow, not wanting to hand over the contents just yet. "Come in."

The door pushed open. Bronson leaned against the frame, freshly showered, and dressed in a dark gray T-shirt paired with blue athletic pants. His messy, damp hair spiked a bit on his head. He ran a hand through the waves, his arm flexing with the movement. Simply gorgeous.

"I changed my mind about the cookies. Wanna join me?" he asked.

She moved from the bed, stood within inches of him and inhaled his fresh scent. Her eyes drifted up his toned chest to his full lips and then met his gaze. Bronson didn't back away or resist her closeness. She wanted to kiss him, but after her last failed attempt, she refrained. Time for him to make the next step.

"Cookies would be good."

He didn't move away and held her gaze a bit

longer than normal. She hoped he'd lean toward her but instead he straightened, then stepped into the hallway. "Lead the way."

Aggie glanced back at the pillow hiding the USB. She'd tell him tomorrow after she had a chance to make a copy and see what information it held. Her mission tonight? Don't fall again for the handsome detective.

SIX

Bronson waited at the bottom of the gym's fifty-foot rock wall and sipped his late-morning coffee. His body ached all over from last night's tumble down the mountain and a lack of sleep, but Leslie was still missing, and he had a lead to chase down. Lee Demsky, who was apparently a regular here at the Power Muscle Gym, hung thirty feet in the air.

Windows circled the top for a three-hundred-and-sixty-degree view for those who were brave or athletic enough to make the trek up the wall to the rafters. Lee was about three-fourths of the way there with no slowing down. The man must be part monkey with the way he swung through the holds.

"Here ya go." The young girl from the reception desk walked over, waving a laminated card in her hand. "I've got your name in the system and since this is a complimentary visit, we allow you access to all the weight areas, the pool—" she motioned toward the climbing structure "—and the rock wall. Plus, you're welcome to visit our VIP lounge with full juice and snack bar on the third floor. Typically, that's for our elite members only but we make an exception for your first visit. There's also a juice bar down here, too, but the lounge upstairs has more options as well as a trained massage therapist. If you join and want those perks, then there's an extra fee."

He took the lanyard from her and slipped the identification badge over his head. "Thanks. I'll keep that in mind."

"If you let me know what you would like to do first, I'll get an assistant to help you. Are you interested in a climb?"

"Me? No. Not today."

"Oh, you should. It's such a rush when you make it to the top." She motioned for one of their spotters to join them. The man sauntered over, the bulge of his muscles impeding any normal walking gait. "This is Butch. He can spot you."

The man grabbed a harness off the station and handed it to him. "Put this on."

"No, thanks. I can't climb today."

"Why not?" Butch asked. "Are you scared of heights or something?"

"I busted up a few ribs last night. Jumped out of a car rolling down a mountain."

The man blinked, hung the harness back on the wall and walked away without a word.

"Guess he doesn't impress easy," Bronson said, a bit deflated at the lack of interest he'd received.

"Okay then." The perky receptionist pointed to the lanyard on his neck. "If you want to get into one of the exercise rooms or check out our Olympic-sized pool, then swipe this where there's a black box and you'll be allowed to enter. Stop back by the front desk if you want me to activate a full membership or to turn in your lanyard before you leave." She walked off with a little wave.

Bronson was more of an outdoors man. He liked getting his exercise in the fresh mountain air with an early morning jog or an evening bike ride on backwoods trails, not in a sweaty gym where too small tank tops where the fashion trend.

The ding of a bell at the top of the rock climbing wall chimed. Lee Demsky descended to the floor. He slipped out of his harness and thanked his spotter before turning toward the main weight room. Bronson followed the man, stepped on the treadmill next to his and exchanged introductions.

"So, you're a detective?" Lee took a swig of his water bottle before dropping it into the built-in holder on the machine.

"That's right. I'm working a case that may have ties to the military."

"Then you're talking to the wrong guy. I'm not a soldier."

"Not anymore, but you work with them."

"I work for Sterling Securities. They contract with the military, among other clients. I don't choose my assignments—I just make sure to complete them."

"And do you? Complete your assignments?"

The man tapped the incline button on the treadmill and kept jogging. "For the most part. I've had a couple of areas that became too dangerous for me to get the information needed, but I managed."

"Anything like that happen in Afghanistan about a year ago?" He gave the date of Corbin's last mission.

Lee started to look suspicious. "What did you say your last name was?"

"Young."

Sweat dripped down the side of Demsky's face. "Any relation to a Sergeant Corbin Young?"

"He was my brother."

Lee shook his head. "Hated what happened to him. He was a good soldier—and an excellent sergeant. But that mission was nothing but chaos. I've never seen anything like it. We covered all our bases. Made sure we surveilled from every possible angle ahead of time. We knew all the marks, entrance and exit strategies, plus we provided an emergency backup plan and he still got killed. I don't blame you for wanting answers. I would, too, if he was my kid brother."

"Did you work with Lieutenant Newton?"

"Aggie?"

A twinge of jealousy sparked from the smile that crossed Lee's face when he said her name. "Yeah. Those were some good days if you know what I mean."

Bronson tapped the stop key on his machine, his side aching from the walk. He inhaled, mostly to keep his sarcasm in check, then leaned against the handrail. "How so?"

"Looking at her was the best part of my day." Lee grabbed his towel and wiped the sweat from his neck while he jogged. "Unfortunately, she had a boyfriend, but we worked on several surveillance missions together. Talented lady. Probably one of the best Black Hawk pilots the army had, but after your brother was killed, she wasn't the same."

If his brother's death had affected Aggie, she never shared her feelings with him. Of course,

Bronson had been too wrapped up in his own grief to notice.

The machine beeped as Lee increased the incline and his speed. *Show-off.*

"We worked a few more missions together but she seemed to have lost her love for her job. And then I heard she retired. Can't say I blame her. That was some firestorm we were in."

Bronson wanted facts not nostalgia. "Do you know the details of my brother's death?"

"No—I only did the surveillance the day before to help them prepare. I usually don't go on the actual missions, but they needed a live camera that night."

"Anything happen that might cause someone to want Aggie dead?"

"Yeah. She and her gunner took out three high-level terrorists to get her troops out of there alive. Revenge is a pretty good motive." Lee grabbed his towel again and wiped his face. "Is Aggie okay?"

"I'm trying to find her twin sister, Leslie. She was abducted yesterday. We have evidence Aggie was the true target."

"I heard about that on the news. Just awful." Lee took another swig of his water.

Bronson shifted his weight. His broken ribs ached with pain from his walk. "What were you doing yesterday?"

The man slowed his pace with the question. "What? You think I took her?"

"We're looking at everyone who was present that night."

Lee pressed the stop key. "I don't even know the woman and have no reason to take her."

"You know Aggie and this is more about her than her sister."

"Then maybe you should be looking a little closer to home," he said and stepped from the treadmill and headed to the weight section.

Bronson followed. "If you're talking about Leslie's ex-husband, he checks out."

"Not the sister." The man grabbed a fifty-pound weight in each hand. "There's only one home Aggie knew for ten years. That's where you need to start."

After a few more questions, Bronson turned in his lanyard and headed back to the office. He grabbed a large cup of coffee, found a small, empty conference room, and spread out all the files across the long oval table. Something in all this was missing and he was going to find the link.

He began listing all of Aggie's team members on the whiteboard when the door clicked open behind him, and Oz entered.

"Any progress?"

"It's slow going. You?"

Oz handed him a file. "I reached out to some of my army buddies and was able to get an unredacted report. Corbin and nine other soldiers carried out the mission that night. Aggie was the lead Black Hawk pilot with another chopper providing weapons support. She flew the unit to their mark and dropped the soldiers on the roof of the interpreter's home."

"What was his name?"

"Vincent Savoy. Your brother's unit cleared the home and returned with the wife and daughter to Aggie's chopper."

Bronson flipped through the pages printed from the case file. "What about Vincent?"

"Your brother was with him as they headed back to the chopper when they came under attack. They were separated from the group by several explosions and heavy gunfire, including rocket launchers. The house went up in flames. Despite all that, your brother got Vincent back to the extraction point."

"Then how was he killed?"

"That part's redacted still. The only part I can read says he was killed in action."

He let the pages fall and closed the file. "Of course. If Vincent's a possible reason for Leslie's abduction, then we need to talk to him. Where is he now?"

"In the States, but my buddy with the US

Marshal's office says they have him in witness protection."

Bronson picked up the blue stress ball he brought from his desk and squeezed. "Great. Another lead inaccessible. Did the report mention if Lee Demsky was involved in the extraction, too?"

"Sterling Securities' employee?"

"Yeah. The army contracted him for surveillance that night. He was the drone pilot. I met him at the gym today."

Oz leaned back in his chair and shot him a look. "You? At the gym?"

"Anything for a case," Bronson said with a smile.

"For a minute there, I was getting worried."

"No need to worry about me, but I think there's more going on here than we're seeing. Smells like a cover-up and I don't like not knowing what happened and exactly why Aggie or her sister are at risk."

Oz pulled out his phone. "Then you might want to talk to your girlfriend again."

"Ex-girlfriend, and why?"

He turned the screen for Bronson to view. "I just got a text from one of our patrols at the house. Said Aggie's headed to the barn with a laptop and USB drive."

Bronson lifted his jacket from the back of a chair and retrieved his car keys from his pocket.

"Where are you going?" Oz asked.

"To find out what she's hiding from me."

Aggie startled awake, either from a loud rumble of thunder or the nightmare still rolling disturbing images through her mind.

Lightning streaked across the sky outside the window of her father's office and lit up the dark room. She reached for the lamp and twisted the switch, but the power was off. The storm must've knocked it out and from the look of the black clouds outside the window, the treacherous weather was not close to letting up.

Rain pummeled the barn's tin roof. She usually didn't mind when nature's lullaby coaxed her to sleep while sitting in her father's old recliner but with time running out for Leslie and the files taking forever to download from the flash drive, she scolded herself for giving into slumber.

She'd retreated to the barn for some privacy. The main house had too many officers inside and she didn't want curious eyes viewing the files before she was ready to turn them over.

One of the patrol officers stopped and questioned her about where she was going but she tried to convince him she just needed some space. She wasn't sure he believed her.

Getting up to stretch her legs, she perused her

father's bookshelf. Volumes on apple orchards lined the built-in case. He loved spending time here, working, reading or organizing sales for their family's produce. He used his old analog radio as a bookend and kept country music flowing through the speakers every day except Sundays. That was God's day and he played worship music or hymns. If they were good girls, he'd whittle scrap pieces of wood into toys for her and her sister. They were still inside a special box her mother kept in her room.

She reached for the radio but pulled her hand back before turning the knob. No use with the power out. An overwhelming absence ached inside her heart and lost time pulled at her emotions. Her surroundings blurred and she had no choice but to settle for the rain's white noise instead of recreating the past.

Aggie closed her eyes, letting a tear slip down her cheek.

I'll bring her home, Dad. I promise.

Her computer dinged, breaking the moment, and she moved to view the screen. An alarm displayed, letting her know that the laptop was running low on battery power, and she clicked the key to continue the process. Sixty percent of the files were ready.

Something cold nudged her hand. McIntosh, named for her father's favorite apple, greeted her with a friendly tail wag. She dug her fingers into his fur while doggy kisses landed on her cheek when she crouched beside him. Aggie raised her chin to keep him from slobbering her lips.

"How's my Mac this morning?" She stared into his copper-brown eyes. "You like it out here, too, don't ya?"

She glanced to his homemade water bowl that her father had hooked up to a water pipe to create a slow cyclic fountain. The constant motion kept his water fresh. He sauntered over, took a few laps, and returned to nudge her hand for more scratches.

"What a great life you have." She petted his head again. The dog came and went as he pleased. Her father had trained him to chase away the deer and other critters from the rows of apple trees on their property. But as Mac aged, he spent most of his time at the farmhouse, sleeping on his cushioned bed her mother had sewn for him. He must've followed her out here and entered through his doggy door.

"Do you miss him, too?"

He padded to the corner where several old horse blankets were piled on the floor and placed his head between his paws. Every now and then, Mac still mustered up a spurt of energy and chased a groundhog or two, but most days he kept to the house or the barn, happy to laze around.

When the dog raised his head, perked his ears, and released a low growl, Aggie paused her work.

"What's up, Mac? You hear something?"

He froze for a moment and then padded to the closed office door. Something thumped against the outside wall.

She glanced at her laptop screen again. Still thirty percent to go. She needed those files to finish downloading.

Another growl came from Mac. Longer this time with a bark at the end.

One of the officers must be coming to check on her. Or maybe a farmhand was finishing up his morning work. Still, it would be smart to check it out. Better safe than sorry.

Aggie crossed the room, opened the door, and stepped into the main aisleway. The length of the barn measured at least one football field, maybe more. Two smaller wings extended on either side and held tractors and equipment in need of repair.

A door to the break room clicked closed across from her. Her body relaxed and she glanced at her watch. Almost lunchtime. "The worker just wants to eat his lunch in peace, Mac."

A crack of thunder rumbled the walls again.

Mac barked and shot past her down the long corridor away from the break room.

"Mac, no. Come back, boy."

The dog kept moving, sniffing the concrete, and pawed at the floor outside the mechanical room her father had used for storage. She still wanted to believe there was nothing wrong, but his behavior alarmed her.

The only reason he would ignore her command and paw at the door is if a stranger was inside. Mac was familiar with all her mother's employees—they wouldn't trigger this kind of reaction. And the police officers would have no reason to poke around inside like this.

She called Mac to return and reached for her weapon. Her holster was empty, and she remembered placing her gun on the desk when she was working. She moved back into the office with Mac at her heels and locked the door behind her. She then lifted her weapon and checked the magazine. Only three bullets. Call her paranoid, but after last night's attack, she needed more firepower than three bullets.

Aggie opened her father's desk drawers and searched for the thirty-eight special he kept.

"Please let it be here." She checked the last drawer and pushed open the false bottom. "Bingo."

She removed the weapon and checked the

cylinder. Fully loaded with six rounds. That would help. Aggie pulled the USB drive from the port with ninety percent of the encrypted files downloaded and logged out of the computer. She wasn't taking any chances on any intruder stealing the information they were after.

The office doorknob jiggled. She spun at the noise. Shadows interrupted the sliver of light underneath the door. Maybe the man from Leslie's house had returned.

Mac stood at attention, ready for her command, and growled. Aggie raised her weapon and aimed, waiting…but no one entered.

She moved to the window and glanced across the acres of pastureland to the main house. Her mother and Holly were inside. She had to make sure they were safe, even if officers were stationed to protect them. She'd never forgive herself if something bad happened.

The shadows disappeared. Maybe they *were* from a worker and he'd returned to his duties. Aggie entered into the main portion of the barn, with Mac by her side, and eased into the first supply room on her left.

Musty boxes of extra parts and empty apple crates filled the shelves. A backdrop they always used at apple festivals hung on the back wall. Aggie kept her weapon aimed as she meandered through the floor to ceiling clutter of the room. No one was there and she exited back into the main aisle.

Her phone vibrated and she jumped at the sudden buzz.

Where are you? Bronson texted.

In the barn.

I'm on my way—we need to talk.

She started to make a run for the exit when a clamor sounded from the next room. Mac lifted his nose, darted to the door, and disappeared into the darkness. She followed.

The space was a bit larger, lit only with the glow from the hallway windows. Her father stored his wood working equipment inside and her mother didn't have the heart to sell his things.

Sawmilled boards of reclaimed wood were stacked against the walls, releasing a scent of pine mixed with cedar. Large equipment, like table saws and planers, filled the floor space while her father's vice and router protruded from a table's edge. Several old sets of horse reins hung adjacent to the door.

They swayed.

Mac yelped.

Her heart rate pumped into her ears and her

breaths grew shallow. Aggie moved farther inside, her weapon aimed.

A man burst from the shadows, knocked the gun from her hands, and shoved her against her father's worktable. The bench slid with their weight, tossing hammers and screwdrivers to the floor. She managed to twist away from him, but with one shove, Aggie landed with a thud and struck the back of her head against the concrete. White dots invaded her vision from the severe pain. He was on top of her, his full weight restricting her movements. She dug her nails into the skin on his face, aiming for his eyes.

"Where's the USB? I know you have it. I saw you through the office window," he said.

Mac growled behind her.

"Attack."

Her dog lunged from the shadows and latched on to the man's arm. He cursed and released his grip on her.

Aggie rolled to her side and groped for the gun. Her hand smacked against the leg of a table saw. Adrenaline dulled the pain and she kept searching for the weapon. Only dirt and hard concrete brushed under her palms. Mac growled behind her, doing his best to subdue the man, but her attacker was stronger.

His muscular arm was around her again, dragging her backward. She kicked and connected with his knee, but even a booted heel didn't stop his assault. He forced her to the floor, straddled her body and used his weight to pin her down.

She couldn't breathe and all the training she learned in the military wasn't enough to compensate for the total lack of leverage. With one hand, he restrained both of hers above her head and leaned in close. His wintergreen breath was hot on her neck, and he patted down her body, before stopping at her front jean pocket. He wanted the USB.

He shifted his weight to retrieve the drive, loosening his grip on her left hand. She couldn't let him take it. The USB was the only bargaining chip she had to protect her sister.

She reached to the side, searching for any object to use as a weapon. Her hand landed on a hammer. She lifted and swung for his head.

He groaned and grabbed his shoulder but retaliated with another backhanded strike across her jaw. Her lip split with a metallic taste. She swung again, but this time, he intercepted the blow and ripped the tool from her grip. Metal clanged when he threw it against the wall.

His fingers tightened around her throat, and he squeezed tighter. White dots pricked the edges of her vision. She didn't want to die. Not like this.

SEVEN

Bronson sped through the streets of Mills Creek, rehearsing every word he planned to say if Aggie tried to keep the USB from him. There were likely classified files on the drive—but since the people who had abducted Leslie were so desperate to get their hands on them, he couldn't do his job without seeing the information. He turned down a side road without even looking at the Newton Apple Farm sign alerting tourists they still had 4.8 miles to go.

Lightning flickered around him, and heavy rain pummeled his windshield. He slowed as he rounded the curve toward the bridge. A man in a trench coat and fedora jumped out of the way as Bronson made the turn. An abandoned car, with the white handkerchief tied to the door handle, was parked behind him. Bronson checked the traffic, made a U-turn in the middle of the road, and rolled down his passenger side window. His conversation with Aggie would have to wait a few more minutes.

"Need some help?"

"Yeah. My car broke down at the bridge and I'm at least a mile from the closest gas station. I could really use a ride."

"Get in." Bronson unlocked the doors.

The man climbed into the passenger seat, soaked three-piece suit and all, then extended a wet hand. "Palmer Sterling. Thanks for the lift."

"Aren't you the CEO of Sterling Securities?"

"The one and only."

Bronson didn't believe in coincidences and silently thanked God for this unforeseen opportunity. "Where you headed?" He suspected he already knew the answer.

"Newton Apple Farm."

"Same place as me." Bronson steered back in that direction. "You need me to call a tow or someone else for you?"

"Already did, but my employees are about an hour away and I got tired of waiting. They'll call our car service and have them pick the vehicle up."

"I can take you to Aggie's place." He dropped her name deliberately, hoping to gain some insight into Palmer's new interest in her.

The man removed his hat and shook off the

water into his floorboard. Bronson reached into his console and handed the man a hand towel he kept for rainy days.

"Thanks." He wiped his face first and smoothed back his straight dark hair. "I don't think I caught your name."

"Detective Bronson Young. Good to meet you."

"You're a cop?"

Bronson figured the man would probably rather be walking in the storm than sitting in his passenger seat—but short of jumping out of the car while it was in motion, Palmer was stuck with him now. He planned to use the time to his advantage. "Just like my father and grandfather before me. I guess you could say it's a family tradition."

Bronson hit the blinker and detoured onto a slower route to give him more time for questions. "Why are you headed to see Aggie?"

"When a Black Hawk pilot returns to Mills Creek, I'm interested. My company is always looking for premium talent and I offered her a job, but she hasn't responded. I'm hoping to convince her to take the position, especially after meeting her in person. She's stunning."

Bronson kept his agreement quiet. She *was* stunning and so much more, though he found the notion kind of cringeworthy for a man to say about someone he planned to hire. "Your company employs Black Hawk pilots? That's impressive."

"We're contracted with the government, so employees who have a military background and training can provide a lot of added value." Palmer folded the towel into a neat square and continued.

"Besides, the veterans we hire have often struggled to find purpose after they come out of the army. They're used to being a part of something larger than themselves, and working for a company who keeps Americans safe provides the purpose and camaraderie they're looking for. Going back to a nine-to-five job for some of them doesn't cut it. We offer them a chance to continue the same kind of work from their military career, but with a better salary."

"Is that why Lee Demsky joined your company?"

"Lee Demsky? He hasn't worked for us in years."

Bronson slowed for the single lane bridge that crossed Mills Creek. The river was rising and spilled onto the road a little. If the storm kept up, no one would be able to cross. "Not even last year for a mission in Afghanistan?"

"I'd have to check my records, but I'm pretty sure Lee's been freelancing for the past two years. Sometimes we hire him to do extra contract work for us, but we haven't needed him lately. I hired two veterans last year to perform the bulk of our surveillance work. They were familiar with the latest technology. In comparison, Lee's knowledge was a bit outdated."

Bronson turned down the paved drive marked by an overhead entrance sign that displayed the family's name. Palmer's statements contradicted what Lee Demsky had told him. Someone was lying and he had to figure out who and why.

Rows of trees filled fenced-in acres of property leading to the beautiful white farmhouse and adjoining store. The white barn, where Aggie was, sat another half a mile away, perched up on a knoll.

Palmer leaned forward. "Is this it? Wow. A beautiful place for a beautiful lady. Aggie's not seeing anyone, is she?"

Bronson stepped on the gas a little harder, the force pressing Palmer back against the seat. "Aren't you planning on hiring her?"

"If she agrees. If not, then I'm planning to ask her out. A win-win, don't you think?" He held up his hands. "Unless of course, you two are—"

"We're just friends," Bronson said.

Truth be told, he wasn't sure what they were.

He was just trying to keep her at arm's length and get through the case while ignoring his persistent feelings for her. Her return raised lingering questions of what could have been, had he tried to work things out or done something different.

He slowed and crossed the arched bridge leading to the main part of the property. "That's the main house and store."

Bronson had spent many days here during his college years, helping harvest the apples and trying to convince Aggie to date him even though she planned to enter the army after graduating from college. She wanted to focus on her military career and not a relationship, but that hadn't stopped him from trying.

He pulled into a parking space outside of the Newton Apple Store. "Here we are."

"This place is amazing. No wonder Aggie wanted to return to her family farm rather than taking my job offer. I'll have to increase her salary to get her to leave all this."

"You really don't know a thing about her, do you? Giving Aggie more money won't convince her to leave her family. She's not that kind of woman."

Palmer hiked up his collar and gripped the door handle. "Even better, but there's one thing I've learned from running my company. Everyone has a price." He pushed open the door. "Right now, though, I think a cup of hot cider is exactly what I need."

Bronson stared after the man as he made a dash for the front door. He should have probably told him Aggie was in the barn, but why would he want to help a wealthy man like Palmer who threw money at his problems and often got everything he wanted? Bronson just hoped Aggie wasn't going to add herself to the list.

He couldn't wait to slap a pair of handcuffs on the man's wrists, but until he had enough evidence for an arrest, he'd let him enjoy his hot beverage inside the store. Besides, he needed to talk to Aggie alone. Bronson retrieved his phone, tapped her number, and frowned when the call went straight to voicemail.

Aggie locked her attacker's arms, thrust her hips upward and rolled him to his back, then punched his face twice. She pressed up and ran for the door, but he grabbed hold of her foot, jerking it hard to make her fall. She dropped with a slam, her breath knocked from her lungs. He pulled her back into the room.

Concrete scraped at her skin and she twisted, striking two booted heel kicks to his shin. Her attacker stumbled back, releasing his grip. She stood, faced him, and lifted a wrench from her father's tool bench. Light from the door outlined his shadow as he charged her.

Aggie stepped to the side and swung. The wrench connected. Bones cracked and the man dropped to his knees. Mac charged at him again, sinking his teeth into the man's right shoulder as he hit the ground. He sprawled unconscious at her feet. She crouched beside him, just as the power returned. After she flipped the light switch, Aggie ripped off the man's mask. She'd never seen him before.

Her adrenaline crashed, blurring her vision as pain and exhaustion took over. The room spun. Aggie sank to the floor and rolled to her side, trying to get her blood back to her brain. Instead, the ringing in her ears increased and blackness invaded the corners of her eyes.

Before heading to the barn, Bronson knocked on the patrol officer's window. He wanted an update on how things were going. The man pointed to his phone and mouthed the word "captain." Bronson stepped away to give him some privacy.

The white farmhouse, perched on a grassy knoll and encircled by a beautiful wraparound porch, was the crowning jewel of the Newton Apple Farm. The large store, attached by an enclosed breezeway, sold all kinds of apple-related goods and gifts.

Palmer sat next to one of the windows at a small table with a steaming mug in hand, charming the pants off of Aggie's mother. A warm fire flickered behind them painting the perfect picture of a gentleman. Bronson didn't buy his act.

The front screen door opened. Holly ran out and gave Bronson a big hug. "Have you found my mommy yet?"

His heart sank with her question. "We're still looking and hope to find her soon. You keep praying for her, okay?"

"I pray all the time. God will bring her back to me."

He wondered how many other children had prayed the same prayer for their families without getting the answer they wanted. He believed God could save her mother if that was His plan, but Bronson knew sometimes God allowed life to play out in ways he didn't understand or want. Especially when they lost ones they loved.

He learned a long time ago to pray and accept the life God gave him, instead of questioning, while loving the people who remained. Including Aggie.

"I'll keep praying, too," he said. "Have you seen your aunt?"

Holly raised her arm. "She's in the barn."

"Still? I figured she'd be back here playing with you by now." Bronson looked across the field at the massive structure. He and Aggie often spent time inside when they dated. Picnics, long talks, and horseback rides kept them busy. She liked to go there to think away from all the hustle of tourists. "How long has she been in there?"

"I don't know." The little girl turned and pointed to one of the second-story windows. "I was up there."

"I guess that's a pretty good view."

Holly nodded, bouncing her curls. "You can see everything."

"Did she go by herself?"

"At first. Then a man went in after her."

Her words cinched his breath for a moment. "A police officer?"

"He wasn't wearing a uniform."

He took her hand and led her back onto the porch. "Let's get you inside with your grandma. Tell her to lock all the doors. Okay?"

"Okay, but don't tell her I was spyin'. She doesn't like it."

Bronson took the steps two at a time after the dead bolt clicked behind him. He opened the officer's passenger door and slid into the seat. "Call's over. We've got a security breach. Call for backup to guard Mrs. Newton and Holly."

The officer started his engine. "Where are we going?"

"The barn."

A cloud of gravel and dirt spun into the air. Bronson looked behind them in the side mirror. Palmer Sterling stepped outside the store's entrance with his phone to his ear.

"No sirens or lights. We need the element of surprise if we're not too late."

"Got it."

The officer rolled to a stop on the upper side of the barn where there were fewer windows. A chain of loud barks rang out from inside when they stepped from the car. Bronson motioned for the other officer to go around to the back exit. He pulled the handle of the main door, but it was locked.

The adjacent window was secured, too. Everything was dark except for a faint glow spilling from underneath one of the room's doors. He scoured the ground, grabbed a rock, and waited. When the dog barked several times in a row, he broke the glass and unlatched the window, then crawled inside. Mac rushed to his side and licked at his hand.

"Good boy." Bronson gave the dog a quick pat, then moved forward.

Several green and yellow tractors provided cover as Bronson crept through the space with his weapon aimed. The other patrol officer entered through a back exit and met him in the middle outside the closed room.

With a nod, the officer kicked open the entrance. Before they could move inside, a large man plowed into them and knocked them both to the ground. Bronson rolled to his stomach and fired a couple of shots. The man staggered. Blood dripped from his right fingertips.

"Mills Creek PD. Don't move," Bronson said, rising to follow.

The man tried the door, but it didn't budge. Bronson squeezed the trigger and allowed one round to hit a target to the left. The man raised his arms into the air.

"On your knees, now."

The intruder knelt and placed his hands behind his head. The officer rushed forward, cuffed the man's wrists, and helped him to his feet. Bronson approached, assessing the man's two-inch gash on his head. "What happened here?"

"Broad hit me with a hammer."

He searched him and retrieved the USB drive from a pocket. "Call an ambulance. He's going to need stitches and an assessment before processing."

Bronson walked back to the room the man had exited. Aggie was still there. She sat against the wall, her eyes closed and head resting back. Bruises circled her right eye, and her lip was swollen with a nasty cut. Mac rested his head on Aggie's leg.

"Looks like he did a number on you."

Her eyes opened a bit and Bronson crouched beside her. Blood matted strands of her dark hair together. Her face was pale, her pulse normal. "Did you get him?"

"We did. He's in custody."

"He's got the drive." She touched her lip and pulled back bloody fingertips, then wiped the residue on her jeans.

Bronson dug into his pocket, retrieved the USB, and held it up. "No, he didn't. Found the drive in his pocket. He's getting stitches when the ambulance arrives and then will be taken to the precinct for processing."

She rested back against the wall and closed her eyes. "Thank You, Jesus. I thought for sure Leslie would be dead by nightfall without that USB."

The other officer stuck his head into the room. "First responder is here, and reinforcements are five minutes out."

"Thanks, man. Can you bring me a first aid

kit, too? I'll clean her injuries while he tends to our suspect"

She started to press up from the floor. "I can walk back to the house."

He placed a hand on her arm. "Stay still. Let's just take a beat. Okay?"

She relaxed again and touched the back of her head. "He hit me with something hard."

"Let me see." She turned around and he brushed her hair around to the other side of her neck. "You've got a good knot and a cut."

The officer returned and handed him the kit. Bronson found the supplies he needed, donned a pair of gloves, and then ripped open the packaging. "Lean forward. I'm going to put some Betadine on it, but you're going to need a couple of staples."

Sirens sounded in the distance. He'd have the paramedics take her to the ER once they arrived. "Why didn't you tell me?"

"Tell you what?"

"That you found the drive."

She winced when he dabbed her cut with the cleaner. "I needed to know what was on the device. If there was classified information about the details of our military missions, I planned to turn the evidence over to the army."

"So, there's nothing tying all this to the military?"

"I don't know yet. The files are encrypted, and the intruder broke in before my software had a chance to crack all of them, so I'm going to need that back." She held out an open palm.

"Since we can't be sure what's on the drive and it's clearly tied to Leslie's abduction, I'll have our cybersecurity team retrieve the data and keep everything confidential. If we find military information on this, we will turn it over either to the FBI or CID. But until then, it stays with me. Besides, the paramedics are here, and you're their patient." He helped her to her feet and escorted her to the ambulance.

That afternoon, Bronson walked down the hall of the Mills Creek Police Department and stopped in front of the interrogation room. He scrolled through the intruder's rap sheet. The man had a record for breaking and entering, trespassing, and felony assault.

Aggie rounded the corner and almost bumped into him. "I was looking for you."

"I thought you were at the hospital." He'd left her in the capable hands of a paramedic with full expectation that she'd be taken to the ER.

"I went, got staples, and left. I'm not going to sit there all day when I'm fine. Besides, we have a suspect to question."

"Correction. *I* have a suspect to question.

You need to go home and rest." He placed a hand on the doorknob and waited.

"I need to find my sister. I'm going in with you."

Many cops liked having a partner during interrogation, but Bronson preferred questioning his suspects alone. There were no interruptions, and he almost always made the criminals talk. "You can't go inside. Mills Creek PD policy. Plus, I don't need him gloating over the bruises he put on your face."

"Come on. I used to interrogate war criminals in places not near as nice. This guy's a lowlife. I can handle him."

He folded his arms across his chest. "You were a helicopter pilot."

"They sent my team to extract some highly guarded operatives. I'm trained in military interrogation tactics just in case a hostage situation occurred."

"This man also assaulted you. I don't need him trying to finish the job or distracted because you're in the room. He might even hold back on information if you're there. We need everything we can to find your sister before it's too late. You can watch from behind the glass."

He pointed to an adjacent door labeled Observation 1, and after a brief moment of hesitation, she moved in that direction.

"He knows where my sister is. Make sure you get the location."

"Not my first time."

"I know." Aggie placed a hand on the knob but paused. "Are you sure I can't help? I do a mean bad cop."

"If I change my mind, I'll motion you to come inside. Until then, let me do my job."

He opened the door and stepped into the interrogation room. The space was small and bare, with white, cinder block walls. The only color was the dark gray rubber molding acting as a baseboard.

His suspect was handcuffed to a secured metal table, stained with coffee cup rings. The man didn't look at Bronson when he entered and pulled the navy hood farther down, hiding his face. He couldn't be more than twenty-one years old, with tattoos inked on each knuckle spelling out the words "Game Over."

Bronson walked to the end of the table, still tender from his previous trauma, and put his laptop down. "I'm Detective Young. Looks like you have quite a few priors, Alfonso. B&E, trespassing, assault resisting arrest and, my personal favorite, assaulting a police officer."

"You got in my way."

"And I'm going to stay in your way until you tell me why you attacked a decorated army lieutenant today." Bronson pulled out a chair, letting the legs scrape across the tile floor, and took a seat.

The man pushed back his hood from his head. He had a snake tattoo on the side of his neck, fangs curving over his sharp jawline. "I ain't got to tell you nothin'."

"You could go that route, stay silent and call a lawyer. If you even have one." He opened a social media image of Alfonso's girlfriend and daughter, then turned the monitor for the man to see. "But with this being a third assault on your record, we're going to charge you. Judges don't like patterns. They send repeat offenders away for long periods of time and this sweet little girl right here—" Bronson pointed to the screen "—she'll be visiting her daddy in jail."

The man straightened in his chair and leaned forward. "Only if I'm convicted."

"Oh, I'll make sure you're convicted. I'll be testifying on the stand in your case. The district attorney and my team have a high success rate of convictions. Your case will be no different." Bronson held his gaze. "Besides, with your history, jail time is almost a given."

The man slumped back in his seat. Bronson turned the laptop back around and opened his report page. "Or you can help us find who's behind all this. My guess is you needed some extra cash and decided to take the job. Who hired you?"

"Yeah, right. I ain't talkin'."

"I need a name, or I can tell your baby mama you aren't coming home for a long time." Bronson snapped the laptop lid shut, picked up the folder and walked toward the door.

"If I give you a name, then I won't see my little girl again."

Bronson stopped midstride and faced him. "Explain."

"They kill snitches."

He took a seat again. "Just by being here, they'll consider you a snitch. They'll never trust that you didn't talk. You're a dead man unless you help us."

"I think I'll take my chances in a holding cell."

"Not if I decide to release you. Then they'll be *sure* you're a snitch." Bronson hoped his bluff worked. He was the only one who might have an idea of Leslie's location.

Alfonso sat up straighter, his restrained hands tightening into fists. "If ya put me back out there, then I'll be dead by midnight. You ain't seen what they do."

"A bullet to the head?"

"I wish. People who hire me ain't kind when their loyalty is betrayed. They ain't above usin' torture or threats against the people we love to keep us from helpin' the police."

Bronson paced the room for a moment and stopped to look into the two-way mirror. He could only imagine what must be running through Aggie's head after hearing the man's experience.

Her sister was being held prisoner by the same ruthless people who had the tough, intimidating man looking scared out of his wits. If he wanted to gain more information, Bronson had to give him a reason to work with him.

"There's a hundred others out there that'll come for her," the man said, pointing at the two-way mirror as if he knew Aggie was behind it. "And they ain't gonna stop with her and her sister. They'll take out her mother and the little girl, too. Especially for the price they're offerin'."

"How much?"

"A hundred thousand."

Bronson returned to his seat, his chest tightening at the amount. "I can protect you and your daughter if you help us find her sister. Where are they keeping her?"

"That kind of info don't come to me. I only know he has her."

"Come on, Alfonso. You've got to do better than that if you want us to keep your family safe."

"I ain't got what you want."

He opened the folder and held up a plastic baggie. "Okay then. What's on the drive?"

"Don't know."

"What *do* you know?"

"They ordered me to kill her after I got it, but I ain't no murderer."

"No. You just beat women up to get the information you need. That's so much better."

"Hey, she fought back. All I planned was one hit, but she kept comin'." Alfonso shifted in his seat. "We get our orders and carry them out. No questions asked."

Most criminal organizations kept their low-level operatives in the dark about who was in charge or the higher-level processes involved so investigators who managed to bring them in were unable to discover the anonymous leaders driving the business. If the hired hitmen got caught, they didn't have any pertinent information to disclose.

"So, you never talked to the man who hired you?"

"Nope. I ain't ever seen him."

"How do you get your assignments?"

"Through a text."

Bronson scrolled through a couple of screens on his laptop again. "But we didn't find any texts about your activities on your mobile phone."

"Cuz, you got the wrong one. My work cell's at home."

"And how does Palmer Sterling fit into all this?"

The man leaned forward. "Palmer who?"

Bronson looked up from the keyboard. He was more convinced than ever that Sterling was behind this…but Alfonso seemed confused. Either he was good at controlling his body language or he was telling the truth. Maybe he really wasn't aware of the man behind the curtain. "Our evidence implicates him."

"And you trust your evidence?"

Bronson studied the man. "Are you saying our intel isn't accurate?"

Alfonso just shrugged. "You're the investigator, man. You tell me. None of that means nothin' to me, anyway. Why they're after someone, what they want… I'm better off not askin'. Ya get too curious, then ya end up dead. When they tell me to do a job, I don't ask questions. I just do it. Doesn't matter to me as long as I get paid."

"You said earlier you're not a murderer."

"That's right."

"You ever have to kill anyone?"

Knuckles on his laced fingers whitened. The snake bobbed again. "They think I did."

"What does that mean?"

"I didn't want to kill nobody so I faked his death."

"How'd you keep them from finding out?"

"My sister's real good with makeup. We told the guy and took some pictures. He cooperated, then left the country. Last I heard, he's livin' on some beach under a new name. If I'd been smart, I'd gone, too."

"What's his new name?"

Alfonso laughed. "Like I'd know and even if I did, what's in it for me?"

"Your daughter gets to live. You were the one who said they'd kill her."

He twisted a small gold ring around his pinky. "I ain't gonna give out that kind of information, not without somethin' on paper."

Bronson reopened his laptop. "I'll talk to the DA, but I need to show that you're cooperating with us. What was your target's former name? Surely, you can tell me that. Even the hit was put out on him with his former identity."

The man tapped his fingers on the table as if he were contemplating his options. "Vincent Savoy."

"The interpreter for the military?"

The man nodded. "May he rest in peace."

"But he's not dead."

"Exactly."

Bronson refrained from punching the guy. "Who ordered the hit? If he's willing to take out Vincent, then he'll kill the victim he has now. Give me a name."

Alfonso fidgeted. "Why do you think I know it? It's not like I'm swappin' Christmas cards with these guys. They don't tell me their names."

"But you know this name, don't you?" Bronson pressed, following his gut. "Maybe you knew him before? Or maybe you found out his name later, but you do know it, don't you?"

"I can't," Alfonso said. "He'll kill my family."

"We have witness protection and can put all of you in touch with our US Marshal services today. Give me the name."

The man's jaw tensed again. The inked snake stilled for a moment, as if preparing to strike. "Captain Ray Mitchell."

EIGHT

Aggie slammed the observation door and jogged down the dull gray hallway of the Mills Creek Police Department to catch up with Bronson. A rowdy prisoner in a nearby holding cell whistled. She ignored him.

"He's lying," she said.

Bronson slowed his steps. "I've interrogated many criminals. I know when I'm being lied to. Trust me, he's not lying."

"Ray would never be involved in any illegal weapons deal, much less order a hit on one of our interpreters. He's honest, one of the best soldiers I've ever met and operates by the book."

"You were friends in the army. You're biased."

Aggie followed him into the bull pen. Several officers looked up from their paired desks. Except Oz. He was already standing and handed Bronson some papers when he approached.

Aggie stepped around him. "I am not biased. I know him. If he wanted someone dead, he'd do it himself. He'd never pay for a hit."

Bronson paused at her revelation and took a sip of the coffee from the cup left on his desk. "So, he *is* a killer?"

"That's not what I meant."

"But he was there with you that night in Afghanistan, wasn't he?"

"He came with his unit, yes, but—"

"Then if he's the one who pulled the trigger, accident or not, he has motive to abduct Leslie. It's my job to call in federal agents to question him regarding any crimes committed overseas." He rifled through the papers Oz handed him. "But I need more than the unreliable word of a criminal when I call in the Bureau."

He grabbed his laptop bag from the back of his chair, inserted the computer inside, then slipped on his blazer and retrieved his keys.

"Oz, do you mind running a full background on Captain Ray Mitchell? I want to know everything he's been doing since he's stepped foot back in North Carolina. All his locations leading up to Leslie's abduction. If he breathed the wrong way, I want to know about it. Also, I want to know more about Vincent Savoy. According to our rat in there, he faked the interpreter's death. Where's this guy now? I doubt its some beach like he said. If we find anything tied to Leslie's abduction, then we need to bring him in for questioning."

"Will do." Oz took a seat back at his desk and started typing.

She followed Bronson from the bull pen and toward the side exit. "Where are you going?"

"To visit Ray."

"You just said that's the Bureau's jurisdiction."

"It is, but to get them here, I need more answers if we're going to find Leslie. Since her abduction is tied to all of this, it can't hurt to talk to the man."

"I'm going with you."

"I figured you would."

She slid into the passenger seat of Bronson's SUV and didn't say much as acres of farmland passed by her window on the drive to Ray's security business in Charlotte, NC. Aggie replayed every conversation, memory, and op with Ray, trying to make sense of the attacker's information.

"I don't believe Alfonso's story."

"Why's that?" Bronson asked.

Aggie pointed to the lingering bruises on her face. "He's willing to beat me up and almost strangle me but his conscience got the better of him when he was hired to kill Vincent? Please.

They were paying him to do a job and there's no way he recruited his sister to help him fake the murder. That's baloney."

"Does seem like a long shot. You think he really killed Vincent?"

"Alfonso's not going to admit to murdering anybody while sitting in an interrogation room with a cop across the table. If Vincent isn't dead, then it's more likely he escaped and our lowlife killed someone else to make it look like Vincent so he got his payday."

"That's why I kept him locked up until we can get more answers. Hopefully, Ray will be able to shed some light on the matter."

City limits replaced spring pastures, and hilled skylines with concrete sidewalks and corporate towers stood in the distance. Her former captain had always liked urban life—the activity and busyness of people and traffic. She wasn't sure why. The quiet hillsides and mountain vistas appealed to her more, but Ray had a different plan from hers.

He was twenty years her senior and had put in thirty years with the army. When her father passed away, Ray took her under his wing and provided the support she needed when they were deployed. He'd lost his father, too, and knew how personal grief affected a soldier. Even after he'd returned to civilian life, as soon as news traveled about her pending discharge, he reached out and offered her a position on his team. She'd been grateful for the offer but refused the job in order to spend more time with her family.

Bronson slowed the vehicle and glanced several times in the rearview mirror.

"We're still a few miles out. Why are you slowing down?"

"We've got a tail."

Aggie looked in her side mirror. A black Cadillac followed several yards back. "They've been with us for a while?"

"Since we got off the interstate."

The turn signal flicked on and the fancy car took a side street. "They're gone."

"I guess I'm a bit paranoid after everything that happened," he said.

Bronson drove a few more miles down the road and pulled into a concrete driveway and up to a large gate, with a small guardhouse off to the left. The logo for Mitchell Enterprises was welded into the ironwork.

A uniformed guard approached the driver's side window. "How can I help you?"

Bronson flashed his badge. "We're here to see Captain Ray Mitchell."

"Does he know you're coming?"

Aggie leaned forward. "Tell him First Lieutenant Newton is here to see him."

The guard shifted his gaze to her, as if he recognized her name, then clicked the button on his radio and announced their arrival. The gates swung open, and Bronson drove down a paved drive, then parked in front of a two-story building with a glass front. Inside the lobby, a man greeted them.

"I'm Tony, one of the guards here. Captain Mitchell is at the outdoor rifle range on campus. I'll drive you over."

The man led them down a hallway, tapped an ID card across a black box and pushed through a side door. Several golf carts were parked in a row. He chose the one decked out with the logo and colors of the state's best college basketball team.

"Carolina blue. My favorite," Aggie said before sliding into the passenger seat.

They wound around the edge of a building and across what looked like a nine-hole golf course to the back side of the property. Loud pops shot off in succession and echoed across the wooded acreage. A large, covered shed came into view. The guard popped open the console and retrieved two voice-activated headsets and safety glasses.

"These are required."

Once geared up, she and Bronson followed him to the fifth stall. "Detective Young and First Lieutenant Newton to see you, sir."

Ray removed his glasses, placed his M16 rifle on the counter and turned to face them. She'd only seen him once before in civilian clothes and the sight was odd then, too.

His gray polo shirt, dark-washed jeans and brown leather shoes gave him a more modern look that suited his toned physique. Not that the man couldn't rock some army fatigues, even when they didn't seem to flatter anyone. His dark hair had grayed around the edges and a slight five o'clock shadow outlined his jaw. He moved toward Aggie and pulled her into a hug.

"It is so good to see you, Fuji."

"Fuji?" Bronson asked.

"That was my call sign." Aggie pulled back from the embrace. "Once my unit discovered I grew up on an apple farm, they did some research and the name stuck."

"But she left out the part how she saved all our lives during a mission on Mount Fuji." Ray extended his hand. "Nice to meet you, Detective Young. Aggie has told me quite a bit about you from back in the day."

"Likewise."

Ray placed his arm around Aggie's shoulders again and gave her another squeeze. "So,

I heard you discharged, but certainly didn't expect to see you this soon. I figured you'd want to spend some time with your mom and sister before coming to work for me."

"I'm not here for a job," she said.

He pointed to her face. "Does your visit have something to do with the bruises?"

Leave it to Ray to always address the elephant in the room.

"Something like that," she said.

He motioned toward two empty bays next to him and picked up his gun to reload. "Wanna shoot? Always makes me feel better when I can take my anger out on a target. My assistant will bring a couple of rifles or pistols—whatever you like."

Bronson took a step closer. "We're here to ask *you* a few questions. Aggie was attacked today by a hired assassin."

Ray's jaw tightened and he pressed in a couple of rounds into his magazine. "Why would someone come after you?"

"I'm not sure," she said. "We think it might be tied to a mission of ours from before we left the army. The worst part is, they have my sister."

His widened gaze bounced to Bronson and then back to her. "Tell me how I can help. That *is* why you're here, correct?"

"We caught and arrested the hitman who attacked Aggie, then questioned him at the precinct," Bronson said. "He mentioned a name you and Aggie both know. We're hoping you can shed some light."

Ray popped open a cooler and handed them both a water bottle, then twisted off the lid on his own and took a sip. "Sure. Whatever I can do."

"Do you remember Vincent Savoy?" Aggie asked.

"The interpreter?"

"Yeah. The one we extracted from Afghanistan."

"That's a name I haven't heard in a long time." Ray turned and placed his water on the shooting counter and pressed the switch to pull his paper target forward. "What do you want to know about him?"

"Why you ordered a hit on the man?" Bronson pulled his phone from his pocket and scrolled through his notes.

"You're kidding, right?" Ray ripped the paper target from the clip. "That's absurd. Why would I want Savoy dead? I risked my entire team to save the man's life."

"Only you can answer that, Captain," Bronson said, the sarcasm thick in his tone.

Ray grabbed a new target, fastened the paper

to the carrier and flipped the switch, sending it down range. "Seems to me, if that were the case, I would've left him in the Middle East where plenty of people wanted to kill him."

"But that would've gone against orders, and you were eyeing retirement. Couldn't let an interpreter get in your way," Bronson said.

"I didn't kill him." Ray pressed the magazine in the gun and racked the first bullet into the slide with a bit more force than needed. "I don't even know where he is."

Bronson folded his arms across his chest and leaned against a post. "Then tell me about the extraction."

"That's classified," Ray said, shooting off ten rounds in rapid succession, hitting the target's center mass.

Aggie waited for him to finish, then placed a hand on her friend's arm. "I understand your concern about discussing army operations, but we think my family was targeted because of something that happened that night. Please. This is my sister's life."

He eyed her for a moment. "You did save my life in Kabul."

Ray flipped the switch again and they both watched the flight of the paper one more time, then he faced Bronson. "We took in two UH-60 Black Hawks that night and a couple of units to conduct our mission. We were to extract an interpreter and his family then transport the units and target back to our field operation base."

"Sounds pretty straightforward."

Ray put another target on the clip. "Nothing is straightforward when your team is headed into hostile territory, but we had a job to do and my men were some of the best soldiers in the army."

Bronson typed a few notes. "Do you remember a Sergeant Corbin Young on the helicopter?"

"Corbin was with another unit. He had his orders and we had ours. Our job was to clear the building and he was to focus on the extraction."

"Right."

"We received a radio call from another ground unit about some small arms fire around our drop sight once we were in the air. We made it to the roof of our target but enemy combatants shot down the other chopper. After that, chaos erupted. We were taking gunfire on all sides." Ray placed a hand on Aggie's shoulder. "But Fuji got us out of there. You should've seen this girl fly us through the worst nightmare of my career. I wouldn't be here today if it wasn't for her."

"What happened to the troops and the extraction?"

"We managed to secure our target and get them out safely. In total, we lost three souls that night, your brother being one of the casualties."

Aggie waited for him to elaborate about how she veered from the original plan and changed their extraction point, but Ray never mentioned her decision. The one choice that cost Corbin his life. At some point, she'd have to share the details with Bronson but now was not the time to tell the man she still loved that she was the reason his brother was dead.

Bronson rode on the back of the golf cart as Ray drove them back to his massive complex. The two old friends chatted as if Bronson wasn't even there.

"I can't wait to show you the training arena we have, Fuji. You're going to love it. I've purchased all the best equipment and the space is even better than the one at Sterling Securities."

Bronson shifted in his seat and leaned forward. "You've been inside Palmer Sterling's company?"

"Sure." Ray whipped into a parking space, opened a side door for them to enter, then continued down a long, white corridor. "Aggie and I both have."

Her cheeks flushed with color. "We went

a long time ago, when the military first contracted with them."

"The higher ups couldn't go so they asked me, and I took Aggie," Ray said with a wide grin on his face. "Have you heard of the company?"

"Who hasn't?" Bronson stepped inside the elevator Ray had summoned to pick them up. "Palmer Sterling is trying to get Aggie to work for him."

A shadow crossed Ray's face. "You wouldn't do that to me, would you?"

"I'm here to help my mom. That's it for now."

"And then you'll come work for me, right?"

The elevator doors opened to a large arena. "My family's my focus."

Industrial lights hung from the vaulted ceiling rafters and a carpeted running track ran along the perimeter. Bays for archery, indoor weapons training, defensive tactics, and more filled the rest of the space. An octagon for sparring sat in the center of the room along with a variety of weightlifting equipment.

Bronson leaned against the railing and scanned the space. "Nice little gym you've got, Ray."

"Nice? This is amazing," Aggie said.

"Thanks to thirty-three years in the military. I promised myself that when I got out, I'd make sure to honor all those injuries and friends' deaths with something great. Within a year, our firm has secured one of the top spots in the country. Not bad for your old captain, eh?"

"How'd you do everything so fast? You've been out for less than a year."

"I purchased the property about three years ago when the real estate market was low. I poured almost my entire paycheck into the renovations to get everything completed by the time I retired. Mission accomplished."

"As always," Aggie said.

Bronson didn't comment. Instead, he added up a typical captain's salary and couldn't make the cost of what had to be over a million-dollar complex add up. The man got paid well, but not that well.

They took the elevator to the second floor and exited next to a room filled with the latest computer and cybersecurity equipment. Flashing lights on hundreds of servers lined the walls. Bronson noted a tall woman with dark hair and black-framed glasses working inside. She seemed absorbed in her programming. Ray stopped at the door and knocked.

"Katja, come join us in the conference room. I got some folks I want you to meet."

The woman looked at them over the top of her glasses. Bronson smiled, but she remained stone-faced as she returned her attention to her monitor, typed a few more strokes before they moved on to the next room. Mitchell tapped an intercom system and called the others to join.

"Team, this is Detective Bronson Young and Miss Aggie Newton who served with me in the army as one of the best Black Hawk helicopter pilots I've ever known." His hand moved counterclockwise around the group. "This is Uriah, Katja, Clayne and Ziggy. They all have served our country in a variety of ways. I couldn't run this place without them."

They each nodded with a couple of quiet greetings.

Mitchell continued. "My friend here is going through a bit of a crisis and Detective, if you don't mind, I'd like to use our resources to help Aggie find her sister."

"I really can't have you involved in our investigation but thank you for the offer."

Aggie stepped forward. "We should let Ray help. The more people I have looking for Leslie the sooner we'll find her."

Ray took a seat at the head of the table and motioned to a couple of empty ones next to him. "Look at it this way. There may be times when someone outside the police department can go places and do things that you can't or won't do. All legal of course, but we have less red tape to follow. Not to mention my team have skills to locate the woman without tipping off her abductors. Finding Leslie Newton will be our main objective."

He'd never felt inadequate before, but these men and women were skilled soldiers, able to bring down governments and take out terrorists. They'd fired automatic weapons, jumped out of planes, and seen some of the worst humanitarian crises in the world.

They trusted Ray. Like Aggie. If he wanted them to follow his lead, then he'd have to swallow his pride and partner with the man as well.

"I'll have to check with my captain, but I can share some of our intel. We believe Leslie was taken by accident. She's Aggie's twin sister, and we have evidence the abductors are targeting Aggie because of something to do with a past military mission involving Sterling Securities and could be holding her at one of their facilities. We need anything you have on them, facility layouts, building locations and any ties to Middle Eastern criminal organizations. Once I have concrete evidence, I can request federal agents to help with the case."

Ray pressed his hands together and looked at his team. "You all know what to do. Dismissed."

The four team members left them and headed to the large computer room.

Ray pushed back from the table. "They're some of the best researchers I know and while they're busy, I want to show you our latest acquisition," he said, then moved to a cabinet and pressed his palm to another black box before the door clicked open. He grabbed a key fob and tossed it to Aggie.

"What's this?" she asked.

"How long has it been since you've been in the air?"

She handed the key back. "I'm done flying."

Bronson had never known Aggie to refuse to fly. "What are you talking about? You're one of the best pilots out there."

"I used to be. But like I said. I need a change."

Ray pushed the keys back into her hand. "Oh no. You're not getting off that easy. Besides, I need another pilot's opinion."

"Really, Ray. I don't want to." Her face paled and her fingers trembled. "Please. You fly us."

Ray took the key and headed for the outside door, leaving the two of them in the middle of the room.

"What's going on?" Bronson asked. "You've never backed down from flying as long as I've known you."

"I just need a break."

He followed her outside. The weather was nice, and a cloudless blue sky stretched overhead. Winds were light and the temperature had to be in the seventies. She once told him that there was nothing like the peace and joy of flying, but he didn't see either peace or joy in her at the moment.

They crossed a large grassy area to a concrete helicopter pad the size of two football fields. "Wow. A twin engine? She's gorgeous," Aggie said.

Bronson walked around the outside. "How'd you afford such a nice chopper?"

"Our first client was overly grateful for our services. We thwarted an assassination attempt on him and his family," Ray said.

Aggie opened the door and looked inside. "Why did someone want him dead?"

"He accumulated his wealth from purchasing several struggling vineyards and turned them around in a year. One of the former owners didn't like his success, accused him of stealing his property and hired a hitman."

Ray pointed out the instrument panel to Aggie. "You'll appreciate this. All digital with the latest technology."

She hesitated but then climbed into the pilot seat. Bronson joined her on the other side.

"This is amazing, Ray. Quite the upgrade from what we started out in."

"Only the best for my team."

"We have a chopper with the Mills Creek Police Department," Bronson said. "Those guys maneuver through mazes of narrow streets to catch criminals, like threading the eye of a needle."

Ray tapped the cyclic with his hand. "I'm sure your guys are good, but I'm also positive that they don't hold a candle to Aggie. She can do things with a chopper no other pilot can do."

"Really?"

Aggie shook her head. "He's exaggerating."

"Then I think you need to prove it to me." Maybe if Bronson could get her in the air again, she'd reconsider her love of flying.

"Not today."

Ray lifted the pilot helmet and handed it to her. "Show him, Fuji. Besides, you'd be doing me a favor. I'd love to know what you think about how she maneuvers."

"Surely you tested the craft before purchase, didn't you?"

"I did, but it's always good to have another pilot's opinion. I only have another week to return her if I change my mind. Go ahead. Take her up. I'll wait for you on the ground."

Aggie conceded, donned the helmet, and flipped some switches. The whir of the blades increased to a higher pitch and sliced through the air above them. The hum of the machine was deafening without the helmet. Bronson was thankful for the built-in communications.

When she was ready, Aggie raised the cyclic and steered with the controller between her legs. The helicopter lifted, then moved forward, seeping across valleys and vistas of green meadows. Layers of blue mountains, covered in evergreen trees, rose underneath them and Aggie dipped and dove into the valleys, demonstrating her piloting skills. Mitchell was right. She was amazing.

"I think this is the first time I've been flying with you," Bronson said.

"After all the time we dated, I never took you up?"

"Nope, I don't think you did. Probably a policy restricting helicopter dates with a multi-million-dollar government aircraft bought with taxpayer money."

She laughed and seemed to be relaxing. "That sounds about right."

Bronson sat back and enjoyed his thirty-minute tour of Ray's massive property. The man had purchased at least three hundred acres of prime real estate. If his security business didn't work out, he could sell and make enough to live off of until death. "You don't find it odd that Ray could afford such a nice estate on his salary?"

"He always invested well, and the army helps

with loans. If he's got wealthy clients, he could make the payments easy enough. Besides, he said that he bought when the market was low."

Bronson wasn't convinced but let the topic drop while Aggie steered the chopper back toward the large landing pad. She brushed down next to the tops of the trees, still several hundred feet in the air. A reflection in the woods caught Bronson's attention.

"Ten o'clock. What's that?"

Before she could answer, a drone rose and fired shots down the helicopter's left side. Bullets pierced the metal and black smoke billowed from the back. Alarms sounded inside the cockpit. Red lights flashed. The helicopter pitched and spun toward the ground.

Aggie fought to keep control of the craft. "Mayday, mayday. We've been hit with gunfire. Left engine failure. Crash landing imminent."

NINE

The chopper nipped at the tops of the pine trees, spiked and ready to impale them if she failed to regain control. Aggie needed a patch of flat ground, but every area underneath them descended into steep mountainous terrain. She cut the left engine and prayed the right one held a bit longer. Trees cleared and Ray's building appeared in the distance. Loud tones chimed inside the fuselage and the ground came at them fast.

"Here we go. Hold on."

Jolted with the hit, the helicopter flipped onto the passenger side and slid across the sod. Blades chopped into the earth, swirling dust and debris around them. Shards of glass from the windshield cut their skin. Aggie gripped the harness until the craft came to a full stop.

Bronson stirred in his seat and moaned. Small cuts dotted his face. "I think my left shoulder is dislocated. I'm going to need some help getting out."

Aggie pulled off her helmet for a better view of his wounds. His shoulder was positioned at an awkward angle, and he held his arm across his body. She pulled on her harness but couldn't get it loose. Gunshots popped outside the craft and the hum of the drone drew closer. "We've got to get out of here. We're sitting ducks."

Bullets rained across the metal fuselage. Aggie ducked, grabbed her helmet from the floor and placed the mic near her mouth. "Ray, kill the drone."

The unmanned aircraft made a circle and headed back in their direction. Gunfire peppered the ground in front of them. Aggie pressed her body up as far as the harness would allow and unlatched the driver's side door but left it closed to provide protection from the attack. Once the drone passed again, they'd have time to escape through the top with the chopper grounded on the passenger side. She peeked toward the building to get an idea of their running distance. But could Bronson handle a run with his broken ribs and now injured shoulder?

Katja stepped outside through the side door with a rocket launcher and fired at the drone. Her aim was perfect. An orange fireball lit up the afternoon sky. Aggie leaned back against her seat and grabbed her helmet again. "Thanks."

Within seconds, Ziggy—the larger of the male team members—climbed onto the fuselage and looked in through the broken window on the pilot side. "Y'all okay?"

She braced her leg against the console. "Do you have a knife? My harness is jammed."

He whipped out his blade and cut her loose, then she positioned herself to help Bronson. "He's got a dislocated shoulder. I need him out of here, so I can reset it."

Aggie released his harness. "Are you ready for this?"

"Not really. But do I have a choice?"

"Nope." Ziggy said, lifting him from the wreckage. Bronson groaned with the pain. They both helped him inside the building as Ray ran toward them.

"What happened out there?"

"I'll give you the details later, but he's got a dislocated shoulder. Do you have an exam room?" Aggie asked. "Somewhere we can go and pop the joint back in place?"

"Follow me," Ray said.

Ziggy joined the three of them down a back hallway, deep inside the complex. "We've got a medical room back this way with a supply of painkillers. He's going to need something."

"We can give him some meds, but I'll use the Cunningham technique to reengage his shoulder. It's gentler than the older method, where people used to just yank it back in place."

Ray stopped and opened a white door to a medical suite that looked like an operating room. Glass cabinets lined the walls with medical supplies and vials of drugs.

"Wow. You really are equipped with the best for your team," Aggie said.

"Uriah's a registered nurse who used to work in our field hospitals. He designed the entire suite, fully equipped for any emergency. We have every piece of equipment just like a state of the art hospital room. I can call him if you need help."

Ray assisted Bronson onto one of the exam tables in a sectioned off bay to Aggie's right. "I need to go check on the rest of my team. Are you good?"

"We'll be fine."

"When you're done, find me. We need to talk about the crash. I want all the details on the drone."

Aggie walked with him to the door. "I'm so sorry about the helicopter. I have no way to repay you for the cost."

"You survived—that's what matters. Things can be replaced."

"I knew I shouldn't have flown."

"Nonsense. I've got insurance and there's a rumor of an updated version I'd like to purchase." Ray placed his hand on the handle, clearly not willing to hear any more apologies. "My team will be investigating the debris field. We'll gather the pieces of the drone to help figure out who's behind this. I'm guessing our detective might be able to track down the manufacturer, right?"

Aggie glanced back at Bronson who still cradled his arm across his body. "I'm positive he could, if there's any identifiable pieces left after Katja's shot."

"Better for the drone to be in pieces than you, right?"

She nodded. "By the way, on our way in we noticed a car following us. A black Cadillac sedan. Do you mind checking your security feed to see if they crossed onto the premises somehow?"

"Absolutely. We'll check all of our perimeter cameras and find out who did this."

"Thanks. I'm still processing everything. After I take care of him, do you mind if we go up on the roof for a better view of the debris field?"

"Help yourself. Around the corner, third door on your left. You'll need this." Ray handed her an access card. "Swipe it through the black box."

"Thanks."

He closed the door behind them, and Aggie returned to her patient. Pain etched into the deepened lines of Bronson's face and sweat dripped down his temple. She took a seat on the bed and placed the hand of his injured arm on her shoulder, then began to massage the muscles. "Try to relax."

His gaze weighed heavy on her. "Are you going to jerk it back in place?"

"I won't have to if you relax for me. Right now, the muscles in your arm and shoulder are tense and protecting the injury. Once we can get those muscles to loosen and release your shoulder joint, the head of the humerus will move back into the proper place on its own."

She continued to press his biceps, deltoids, and trapezius muscles, trying to keep her mind off of his toned physique. "Any thoughts on the drone that came at us today?" she asked, partially to distract him from his pain and to keep her focused on their mission.

"My guess? The weapon was made by none other than Sterling Securities."

"You think we were their test target?"

"I think whoever wants you quiet, decided to try and kill you today. I was an added bonus."

The joint popped and Bronson's eyes widened. "It went back into place."

She released his arm and wiggled her fingers in front of him with a smile. "Pure talent."

He took her left hand in his and stroked her bare ring finger with his thumb, the symbol of their engagement no longer there. "You saved my life today. I can't think of any other pilot who could have landed the chopper in one piece after an engine failure."

The memory of his proposal replayed in her mind—They'd been together for almost seven years before he got down on one knee during a beautiful ocean sunset. She'd accepted the square cut diamond and couldn't wait to be his wife, but when he ended their relationship, she gave the ring back, not wanting the reminder of their failure.

"Not my first time."

"I'm sorry, Aggie. For everything."

She pulled her hand back, moved to a bank of cabinets and rifled through them for something to secure his shoulder. She found a sling, returned to his bedside and slipped the strap over his head. "Don't do much with this arm for a few days. Since the joint has popped out once and the muscles are stretched, it can happen again until you heal."

"Are you not going to forgive me?"

Aggie fought back the tears burning the corners of her eyes. "I forgave you a long time ago,

Bronson. All that's in the past." She tightened his sling to fit his arm. "I have to focus on my sister right now."

He swung his legs over the edge of the bed and stood. "I wouldn't expect anything else."

"Then let's go to the roof. That's the best place to start. The view from there will allow us to see the entire scene."

They exited and moved down the marbled hallway. Ten-foot walls, dressed with industrial artwork, flanked them on both sides. She found the door, swiped the badge Ray gave her, and ascended the stairs. Once on the roof, they crossed to the low wall surrounding the edge, and found a good vantage point.

"You saw the craft first. It came from over there, correct?" she asked.

Bronson pointed to the right. "When we were in the air, I noticed a reflection at ten o'clock which would be two o'clock from this point of view."

Aggie followed her flight path back to the damaged fuselage. Ray's team walked around the perimeter, taking photos and gathering evidence. The helicopter was a total loss. Her stomach tightened at the thought of what could've happened.

She leaned against the wall and stared at the sun sinking closer to the mountains. "So, they followed us here after all, even though that Cadillac turned off before the entrance."

"They turned down a side street that, I'm guessing, runs along the perimeter of Ray's property. They could've parked and hiked into the area where we were flying."

"They didn't know we'd be taking the helicopter up."

"That drone could have fired at us in the car, on the ground—wherever. They didn't need us to be in a helicopter...but I'm guessing they were pretty happy that things worked out that way. Even if they didn't manage to hit us directly, they were still able to make us crash."

"And what about the timing? Why now? Why here?"

"If you want my guess," Bronson said. "I think the last person they wanted us talking to was your friend. Why do you think that is?"

"Not sure." She watched Ray work with his team. "Unless he knows more than he's telling us."

Bronson took a seat on the wall beside her. "Since your sister's abduction, whoever wants you dead is getting more desperate. I don't want you staying alone. You need twenty-four-hour protection."

"Haven't we already discussed this? I can handle myself."

"I have no doubt, but you don't have to handle everything alone."

She'd seen that look in his eye before. A time when they dated and loved each other. A time before his brother was killed and they'd both built a wall to protect their hearts. If only she'd done more to protect Corbin. Then maybe Bronson wouldn't have ended things between them. But there was no going back.

She bumped his shoulder with hers. "What do you expect? I'm Army strong."

He smiled. "Yes you are, but we'll be stronger together. I think with their escalations, the time has come to put a protective team together until this is over." He took her fingers in his and held them for a moment. "You've always been able to take care of yourself. I guess I hoped you might need me for once."

The air tensed between them. She *had* needed him. A long time ago, when her life turned upside down, but he hadn't been there. The moment turned too real, too fast, and she pressed up from the wall and took a couple of steps. "I do need you. To find my sister."

He didn't let go of her hand. The warmth of his touch pulled her back to him. His fingers brushed the loose strands of hair from her face, making her skin tingle. They never had any issues with physical attraction.

"I have to tell you something," she said.

He leaned toward her ear, his breath sending a shiver through her. "Can't it wait?" he asked, his lips brushing her cheek.

She was able to battle enemy fighters in the Middle East or fly Black Hawks into hotbeds of resistance, but when Bronson Young stood close to her, she turned to putty.

Aggie closed her eyes and swallowed. "I want to tell you everything you need to know about Corbin."

His body stiffened. He slid from his seat on the wall and released her hand. "I thought Ray told me everything."

"He left out a few details."

She shoved her fingers into the front pocket of her jeans, noticing his immediate mood shift. She'd kept this secret too long, but couldn't bear to let him in again, only to have him turn away from her later, when he learned the truth.

Aggie took a deep breath in as the color faded from the sky, giving way to dusky shadows across the mountains. She turned to meet his narrowed gaze.

"Corbin's dead because of me."

Bronson processed her words, trying to make sense of her statement. He'd searched for months for every scrap of information he could find about Corbin's death, and all along she'd been keeping quiet to protect herself?

He held her gaze. They'd survived a helicopter crash, gunfire, and a full-on assault, but nothing stung more than hearing the truth.

"What do you mean?" he asked.

"Like Ray told you, we were under heavy fire and the other chopper had been hit. I had orders to abort, but Corbin wasn't on the helicopter yet, so I delayed take off. The soldiers did an amazing job defending the aircraft during the delay and a few seconds later, I saw Corbin wounded right outside the helicopter. I alerted two of his team members and they pulled him inside before we took off, but he'd already been shot."

"I don't understand how that's your fault."

She dug her fingertips into the top of the concrete wall. "I changed the extraction point before takeoff due to the reports of hostile fire. The move placed us closer to the interpreter's home, but enemy combatants surrounded the area. If I'd stuck to the original plan then he might still be alive."

"Or you all would be dead." Bronson folded his arms across his chest and stared out at the mountains, darkening with the setting sun. "He almost made it out?"

"Almost." She followed his gaze to the half-moon growing brighter with each second. "I guess we were fortunate to have only lost three lives instead of the entire squadron."

"I guess so. I just wish it hadn't been my brother."

"I know this probably doesn't bring much comfort, but he died saving a man and his family. I don't think there is any other more honorable way to go."

"Sounds like Corbin. Always the hero. I just wish you would've told me all this right after he died. Then maybe—"

"There's more." She hesitated. "The bullet the surgeon removed during the autopsy wasn't from our enemy. Corbin was shot with one of our own weapons. He was killed by friendly fire."

Bronson turned, placed his back to the wall and bent forward, then straightened. "No wonder the report they sent me was heavily redacted."

"It was a messy fight. We were taking heat all around. The army concluded he was struck in the crossfire. If I hadn't changed extraction points, then Corbin still might be here, but I wanted to get in and out quick."

Aggie pushed her hands into her pockets. "But with everything that's happened, I'm not sure the shooting was friendly. I think someone might've wanted him out of the picture. Maybe he walked in on something he shouldn't have."

"Did the army conduct an investigation?"

"They did, but there wasn't enough evidence to implicate any of our team members."

"Who was with you that night?"

"There was the aircrew, Ray's and Corbin's units as well as the interpreter and his family."

"Did they check out Vincent, since he was with him when he died?"

"He claimed he didn't see what happened."

"Is that everybody?"

"Also, Lee Demsky. The employee I mentioned who worked for Sterling."

"I thought he was a contractor for them."

"I'm not sure."

He made a mental note to dig into Palmer and Lee a bit harder, maybe even get a search warrant for Sterling's employee records. "They keep popping up, don't they?"

"Who?"

"Sterling and Lee, but neither one of them wants to acknowledge the other. Someone's lying to me, and I don't like it."

Bronson pressed up from the wall and walked toward the rooftop door.

"Wait," Aggie said. "Let's be smart about this. If they are behind my sister's abduction and we go straight at Palmer, I'll never see Leslie again."

"I don't have enough that's concrete to call in the feds yet. Everything we have is hearsay or from the mouth of an unreliable witness. I'm open for suggestions. How do we get one of them to talk?"

"We find out what's on the USB drive."

"It's with my team back at the precinct."

Aggie headed back toward the rooftop door. "Good thing I made a copy then."

He grabbed the handle and kept her from leaving. "When did you do that?"

"I downloaded most of the encrypted files to my hard drive, even though I couldn't open them. Figured it couldn't hurt to have a copy or two for leverage. I knew at some point I'd have to hand the drive over to the army or—"

"Me?"

"Don't be mad. I wasn't about to risk losing Leslie because I didn't have the files."

Bronson leaned against the door. "I'm not mad. Actually, I would've done the same thing had I been in your shoes." He smiled. "Guess who has a really high-speed computer and a cyber genius on campus."

Aggie smiled back. "Ray."

TEN

Bronson poured a steaming hot cup of coffee and popped two ibuprofens into his mouth. The helicopter crash from earlier aggravated his still-injured ribs, and he was aching all over. He savored the aroma and prayed the pills would kick in soon.

Aggie walked into the large lounge area and filled a mug, too. "I just got a text from Ray. Katja has cracked the encryption on the USB drive and he wants us to meet him in the computer room."

"Man. She's good. I'll let the precinct know. We had a little competition to see who could get there faster but looks like Ray won."

"That's what happens when a hacker owns the most sophisticated computer system out there," Aggie said.

They walked down the white corridor, took the elevator to the second floor, and entered the room.

The entire team was there, seated around a long table and staring at a massive screen on the wall. Aggie and Bronson grabbed their seats.

"Okay, Katja. Show them what you found," Ray said.

"We were able to crack the encryption and I've been going through the files. They all contain schematics and documentation of classified weapons made by Sterling Securities. There's still more to go through but I wanted to show you something specific I came across."

She pulled up a diagram of a familiar structure.

Aggie leaned closer. "That's a schematic of the new Black Hawk helicopter design being tested. The government hasn't even released it for use yet."

"How did you know about it?" he asked.

"I was given the opportunity to test one. Everything was confidential and classified."

"Any idea how secret information ended up on a USB drive?"

"Not from the army. They lock down classified information like Fort Knox." Aggie motioned to the sidebar that held a list of all the files. "Can you open these?"

Katja obliged. "They're all diagrams of proprietary weapons used by the military."

"And they all belong to Sterling Securities,"

Bronson said. "Ray, do you recognize these models?"

He stood and walked closer, pointing to the corner of one of the diagrams. "They all have signatures of approval on them. Can you enlarge this area, Katja?"

The small script, too tiny for the normal eye to read, centered and zoomed on the monitor. Bronson searched the names listed in the small box. Most he didn't recognize, but the one name he hoped for was there. "Palmer Sterling."

"Makes sense. His company created the diagrams," Aggie said. "He would be required to sign off on them."

"True." Bronson still needed more.

The woman opened a few more screens. "Wouldn't be hard for one of his employees to gain access to the files and download them from the company's network while he's here in the States, then simply transport them overseas via a USB or external hard drive. He then contacts his connections and makes a deal."

"Costing hundreds of lives in the process," Bronson said.

Aggie leaned back against the counter. "Soldier's lives at that. When we go into a hot zone, we usually have the upper hand with our equipment, but if terrorists are purchasing our schematics and manufacturing the same weapons, then it's like we're fighting against ourselves—especially since they know any vulnerabilities we may have. There's only one problem."

Bronson straightened. "What's that?"

"The government doesn't allow any external drives to be used with their computers. If anyone was seen with a USB, he'd be questioned."

"Maybe that's why the drive was left on the helicopter. If the deal didn't go as planned, he couldn't take a chance of getting caught with it."

"Take a look at these." Katja stepped away from the monitors. "I found an email account tied to the negotiation. Whoever is selling the schematics uses the draft folder to communicate with the buyer. These messages were never sent."

"They read more like a contract," Aggie said. "This is the way they set up their buys. No wonder they wanted this drive. If we can match these emails to the logins used, we would have the seller and the buyer's identity." She leaned over to Bronson. "Would that be enough concrete evidence for you?"

"Just to make sure I'm clear, the buyer logs in to this email account, types up his message, and leaves it in the draft folder, never hitting send. Then the seller checks the account and responds with another draft email."

"That's correct," Katja said.

"Simple but brilliant." Bronson shook his head. "Katja, what about other logins to the account. Is there a list that would give us all the buyer's names?"

"Not that I could find. Looks like they used one email account per buyer. Different email accounts with each transaction would keep the sales from being connected and they could delete them after each sale. However, since this sale never finalized, the account is still open, and I was able to track the logins to three different Sterling Securities facilities."

The woman opened her GPS software and entered the coordinates. Bronson smiled when the map popped up on the big screen. "Can you send that to me?"

He faced Aggie. "We may have just found your sister."

"But which facility is she in? We can't hit them all at once and if we only target one and she's not there, they'll move her."

"Maybe Vincent or Lee Demsky could provide us with a better idea of the location where they would hold your sister."

"Vincent Savoy?" Katja asked, a bit of concern in her voice.

"Yeah, why?"

"There were a couple of recent messages in the account about him which I thought strange since most of the communications were dated around a year ago, but then they picked back up in the last couple of weeks. He's in danger."

Bronson took a sip of his coffee and read the contents. "They've got a fifty thousand dollar hit on his head?"

"Looks that way. He must know too much to warrant that kind of price."

"You don't know who placed the order, do you?" Bronson asked.

The woman pulled the USB from the side of her computer and handed it to him. "Now wouldn't that make things easy. If I did, of course I would tell you. However, I've set alerts in case anyone logs back in and when they do I'll be able to triangulate their location but until then you're going to have to use good old-fashioned police work."

He took the USB and handed it to Aggie. "Since this contains classified military information, you might want to turn this over to your superiors and give them a heads up that the security of their weapons schematics has been compromised. I can give my copy to the feds when we get back and get a search warrant for Sterling's facility and find out where they are holding your sister."

"You know if I do that, they'll cancel their contract with Sterling Securities and then

Palmer will know we're on to him. That puts my sister in more danger. He won't have any reason to keep her alive."

"True. We don't want to give Palmer the upper hand before I have a chance to raid his facilities. Whatever we have to do to protect Leslie, we will do."

"Then we need to find Vincent," Aggie said.

Bronson's phone vibrated and he read the message. "Looks like we just did." He turned his phone for her to read. "Oz just sent me Vincent Savoy's address."

He stepped outside the room and called his partner. "You got him? Because if so, we need to get him to a safe house."

"Might be too late for that. Looks like they already found him," Oz said.

"What?"

"A call just came in. Shots were fired at his address."

"Is he still alive?"

"Not sure. I thought you'd want to move out with the SWAT team."

Bronson stepped back inside the room. "Ray. Do you have another helicopter?"

"Of course. Why do you ask?"

"Aggie and I are going to need a quick ride home."

Bronson turned his attention back to Oz.

"Get a SWAT team together. I'll be there in less than thirty minutes. And Oz?"

"Yeah, bud."

"We need him alive. He's our best person to tell us Leslie's exact location."

Aggie took her spot in line as the SWAT team prepared to enter Vincent Savoy's residence. She scouted the neighboring yards for any armed suspects. Large lots with midcentury, ranch-style homes lined the street. About twenty houses in all. Other than the glow of a few living room TV sets and a dog barking every few seconds, all was quiet at the late hour. She wanted the same for her sister—home sleeping in her own bed with her daughter in the next room.

A hand landed on Aggie's shoulder.

Bronson fell into line behind her. "Are you ready?"

"Of course."

The officer at the front of the line swung the battering ram at the dark gray door and the team flowed into the space. Aggie moved into the foyer with Bronson and two other teams on her heels. She raised her weapon and took the steps off the main entrance to the second floor while the other officers fanned out below. The floor plans she'd studied before arrival boasted one office, a smaller bedroom and a remodeled master suite positioned above the two-car garage.

She stepped through the first door at the top of the landing and moved inside. A large king-size bed stood against the wall to her right with floor-to-ceiling windows positioned straight in front of her. Bronson aimed his weapon toward the bed while she moved through the room to the adjoining bath.

"Clear," she said.

He emerged from the large walk-in closet. "Clear. Doesn't look like our guy's here."

The other two teams checked the rest of the second floor, then passed by the door on their way back downstairs.

Aggie looked around. "Do you see any evidence of gunfire?"

"Nothing that's obvious." He searched through a few dresser drawers and checked out the items on a nearby bookshelf. "Maybe some of the officers downstairs can give us a bit more information."

"I really hoped he would be here," she shuffled through a few papers on a corner desk but found nothing helpful.

"I'll have a couple officers canvas the neighborhood. There are some security cameras on the outside of the house. Our cybersecurity team can hack into them and review the footage. Maybe something will give us an idea where we can find him."

Aggie walked to the bedroom door. "Do you smell that?"

"Yeah." Bronson closed the nightstand drawer. "Smells like smoke."

She stepped into the hallway and rushed to the end. Smoke slithered from underneath the door. The metal knob was warm but not searing hot.

Orange flames shot up the walls when she opened the door, ascending from the garage below. The hardwood floors were already alight. Black smoke encircled her, obscuring her vision. She tumbled back into the hallway and coughed. "Everybody out. Fire."

Bronson moved closer and she grabbed his arm. "We need to go now."

"There's an extinguisher in the closet."

"The blaze is too big and the flames are spreading quick."

They descended the stairs. Smoke filled the lower rooms as well. She groped for the wall, crouched lower and struggled to find the front door. "I can't see."

Bronson grabbed her hand and pulled her with him. Temperatures inside the home ratcheted up as they moved toward the exit. Another officer rushed inside the entrance and helped them.

"Is everyone out?" Bronson asked the officer.

"Our entire team's accounted for."

"And no one else was inside? No family members?"

"We cleared every room before we saw the flames."

"Has it been called in?"

"Yes, sir. Fire and Rescue are one minute out."

The wail of sirens grew over the roar of the fire lapping up the wood of the home. Aggie inhaled the fresh night air and watched the flames leap into the sky. Another minute or two and they would've been trapped. She took a seat on the ground and lowered her head between her knees, trying to calm the dizziness spinning in her head.

Red lights flashed on the ground around her, and she lifted her gaze to the inferno. Spray from the fire truck's hose sprinkled against her Kevlar vest and resulted in plumes of thick smoke pouring into the sky.

Oz rushed over to her and Bronson. "Are y'all okay?"

"Yeah. Just trying to breathe oxygen again." Aggie rose to her feet and stepped close to Bronson who stared at the burning home without saying anything.

"The origin of the fire was in the garage," Oz

said. "They think we triggered the fire when we entered the structure. Looks like someone wanted to trap us inside."

Bronson crossed the charred property and found the fire marshal. "Is it true? Was the house booby-trapped for us?"

The older man directed his flashlight toward what was left of the only garage wall still standing, charred with black soot. "Looks that way. The fire spread from here on the first floor and traveled up the walls. An accelerant was used and caused the blaze to spread fast, especially since most garages are required to have a fire wall these days to pass inspection."

"This is an older home. So maybe there wasn't a fire wall. If an accelerant was used then the intended occupants wouldn't have had time to escape. This was a hit."

"For whom? Vincent Savoy or us?" Aggie asked, as she joined them.

Bronson shed his Kevlar vest. "Do we know what triggered the flames? If the structure was burning when we arrived, we would've noticed."

"One of the officers saw a white light across the bottom front porch step when y'all entered. He figured the homeowner added an outdoor luminary to highlight the path, but after some investigation, the light was a motion sensor designed to trigger a timed digital laser activating the fire when we crossed the threshold."

"Then Vincent set this up and triggered the flames?"

"Not sure," Bronson said. "But with a fifty thousand dollar hit out on his head, my guess is he booby-trapped the home as a security measure and planned to ignite the blaze if he had to make a run for it. Destroy any evidence he lived there. I just hope we don't find his charred remains in the rubble."

"But our team cleared every room before we evacuated. No one saw another body or person."

The fire marshal inspected the origin of the fire a bit closer. "Let's hope that holds true. My team will find him if he's here. I just pray, if we do uncover his remains, his family's not with him."

Bronson took a call from the cybersecurity team while they waited for more conclusive information regarding the fire.

When the call ended, he pulled his team together. "We hacked into Vincent's security cameras. They have footage of two men entering Vincent's home through the side door. Gunshots were fired but Vincent is seen leaving on foot through the backyard which means he could be hiding in this neighborhood somewhere or even be in one of the houses. We need to find him."

Bronson made a gesture and the teams split up into pairs and canvassed the area.

Fifteen minutes passed, and two patrol officers approached him. "We talked to a little old lady down the street. She wants to speak to the man in charge."

"What's her name?" Bronson asked.

The officer motioned to his right. "Jackie McDonald. She's in the little blue house on the end."

Bronson didn't waste any time and hoped she had a location or at least a direction for Mr. Savoy. Aggie fell into step beside him. "I'm praying she's a nosy neighbor and knows where Vincent is."

He took the front porch steps two at a time, then knocked on the woman's door. "Only one way to find out."

No answer. He pulled open the outer screen and tried again. Still no answer.

"Do you think she's okay?" Aggie asked.

"Not sure, but since she requested a visit, that's what she's going to get. Stay behind me."

Bronson tried the door. Unlocked, so they entered. Aggie stepped to his right and cleared a formal living area while he continued straight toward what looked like an open kitchen. A little white dog ran down the hallway and barked.

"Ms. McDonald?" he said.

The kitchen opened to a large family room with a fireplace. An old nineteen fifties refrigerator hummed in the back corner. Rooster collectibles and country antiques filled every nook of the room.

Bronson turned left and continued down the hall, entering the first bedroom but Aggie didn't follow. Unusual for her not to help him clear a room.

He stepped back into the corridor. She faced him with her hands in the air, unmoving, her gun on the floor. A man stood behind her, his arm around her throat, pressing his weapon to her head.

Aggie ducked her chin to keep her abductor from getting a full choke hold around her neck and kept a tight grip on his arm.

"Put the gun down, Detective, and I won't hurt her," the man said.

She recognized his voice. "Vincent, you don't want to do this."

Other than what she'd studied in the man's file before the extraction, Aggie knew very little about his character, except that he would do whatever was needed to protect his family. If she could appeal to his softer side, then maybe they'd all come out of this scenario unscathed.

"Sorry, Lieutenant," Vincent said, "but this is the only way I can secure my family's safety after hired hitmen invaded my home and burned it to the ground. I don't know who to trust."

Bronson held his hands up in a gesture of surrender. "You can trust us. We're here to help you and hope you can return the favor."

"Like I trusted the man dressed as an officer who showed up with another assassin to kill me? I don't think so."

"They weren't with us," Aggie said.

His grip released from her neck, but he kept the gun to her back. "I can't be going to jail where they'll have someone on the inside willing to take me out for a minimal fee."

Bronson tucked his weapon into his holster. "We can help with that."

"Then let's talk in the living room." He directed Aggie in that direction. "Take a seat."

"Where's Ms. McDonald?" Bronson asked.

"She's safe in her bedroom. I told her to stay in there until I could talk with both of you. The last thing I want to do is bring her into this mess."

Aggie sat on the couch across from Bronson. She wanted to keep eye contact with him through the entire ordeal in case things went south and they needed to move.

Black boots scrubbed across the hardwood floor as Vincent paced, tapping his weapon against his thigh. Sweat beaded on his forehead and his T-shirt displayed pit stains. He seemed more nervous now than the night of the extraction.

"If you tell us who's after you, then we can help keep your wife and daughter safe," she said.

"Sterling Securities."

Their name again. Bronson was right. They kept showing up whenever things turned violent. Aggie shifted on the cushion. "Why do they want you dead?"

"All of my interpretation was for them. I know about every meeting that went down in the Middle East. I know the details of the contracts made—the legitimate ones and the ones off the books."

His eyes were wide when he looked at them and his pacing didn't slow.

"What do you mean 'off the books?'" Bronson asked.

"I guess I have nothing to lose by telling you now. They already have a hit out on me. I certainly owe them nothing anymore."

Vincent took a seat and placed his weapon

on the side table with his hand on top. His knee bounced from the adrenaline clearly still rushing through his body.

"You know that Sterling Securities contracted with the government to supply weapons to multiple branches of the military, correct?"

"Go on," Bronson said.

"What the US government doesn't know is that Sterling Securities collects information about all the military operations they take part in and provides schematics of the weapons to whichever terrorist group offers the highest bid."

He swiped a hand through his thick dark hair, stood again and started pacing. "When a deal is made, the terrorist leaders meet with field representatives sent by Sterling to set up their contracts. That's where they often needed my services."

"Did Sterling pay you?"

"A nice sum."

"And the government paid you, too?"

"Pennies."

"Is that what went down the night Aggie and her team were sent to extract you? Were you the one supplying the interpretation for the negotiations between Sterling Securities and the terrorist groups?"

"You don't understand. I didn't have a choice. They threatened my family."

Aggie had met Vincent's wife and young daughter in the helicopter. The woman had shielded her daughter's eyes from the trauma of Corbin's death and rushed to get off the chopper when they landed at the main operating base. "But we delivered your wife and daughter safely. Why would they come after you on US soil?"

"My services were no longer needed here in the US. My loyalty came into question, and I suppose they became paranoid I would talk. They placed a hit on me, but after they discovered I was alive, I started getting threats. Black sedans followed me, and I'd see the same people over and over again behind me on the street. I got the government to hide my family until this all blew over, but the threats kept getting worse. I planned to join my wife and daughter but didn't want anyone to follow me to our new location."

She shot Bronson a concerned look. A black sedan followed them, too, all the way to Ray's facility and the one thing she'd learned over the last few days is that whoever was behind the attacks, didn't give up.

"You said you negotiated all of Sterling's weapons deals." Bronson leaned an arm across the edge of the sofa, his hand closer to Vincent's weapon. "Do you remember a Sergeant

Corbin Young? You were there the night he died—the night you and your family were extracted. What happened to him?"

Vincent sat back in the chair, his shoulders slumped. "After the explosion, Sergeant Young and I got separated from the extraction team. There was gunfire all around and a group of questionable people who were in the process of negotiating with Sterling returned as we were leaving. They shot him and planned to kill me, too, but I kept my life by giving them a copy of the same USB drive I had given my wife. They spared my life."

Aggie kept an eye on Bronson's movements. If he got a clean swipe, he'd take the gun. Maybe she could distract Vincent. Make him forget about the weapon.

"So, your wife is the one who left the drive in my helicopter? Why didn't she take it with her?"

The man stood and paced again, keeping the gun in his hand. "My sweet Paksima never approved of Sterling. She didn't like that they sold secrets to terrorists, but our goal was to get to the United States. This was the fastest way to earn a lot of cash. I wasn't the one breaking the laws—only interpreting the negotiations. Sterling Securities brokered the deals. I was only communicating what they wanted."

Bronson shifted his weight. "But those deals have killed hundreds, maybe thousands, and they have also put your own people at risk. We're going to need every name of every person you worked with during the weapon negotiations. Don't leave anyone out."

"I have a few names I can supply, but they were often low-level representatives and not top leadership."

"Whatever intel you can give will be appreciated. We'll use it as leverage against Sterling. We believe they've abducted Aggie's twin sister by mistake, and we need everything we can get to bring Leslie back and keep Aggie alive."

Vincent faced her, his look hardened and she noticed a shift in his demeanor. "Do you have the drive with you?"

"Our cybersecurity team has the original device," she said with caution, not telling him she kept a copy with her at all times in case she needed it to trade for Leslie.

Vincent paced the floor again and pointed at Bronson. "You can't trust anything Sterling tells you, even if their words seem sincere. And if they can grab Aggie as well, they won't hesitate to eliminate her. She's like me and knows too much."

His words alarmed her and she gripped the chair handle a bit harder. Bronson noticed.

"I don't think you want all that tied to you," he said. "Put the gun away and work with us. We're all on the same side. I'll make sure you and your family are safe if you provide us with everything you know regarding Sterling Securities. If you don't want to cooperate, then I'll arrest you and take you in."

Vincent tucked the weapon in the back of his pants and took a seat. "I might be able to help you with more than just names. They have a couple of unlisted properties. They keep them off the maps by paying bribes to the city council."

"How do you know about their properties here in the States?" Aggie asked.

"Once or twice, Sterling flew me here on his private jet to interpret some dealmaking with clients who wanted to see the merchandise. I was never allowed into the viewing area but when the negotiations came back to the table, I was the one to communicate the details of the purchase."

Aggie sat forward, stirred by the mentions of private properties, confirming what Katja had found. "What are the locations?"

"Two are in other states but there's one about an hour away in the foothills. Their security is massive, especially for a property that's off-grid."

She shot Bronson a look. "Do you think they're holding my sister there?"

"Only one way to find out."

"I can take you there, if you want."

"We know the location, but do you have an access key?" Bronson asked.

"I can get one, but it will have to be the day of. Sterling changes the security code daily with a notice going out to their employees via a secured text. Or I can set up a meeting. You can use the drive as leverage and then raid the facilities instead of meeting with them. I just hope they don't shoot your sister since they would know you're coming."

Aggie exhaled when Bronson chose the first option—an access badge to enter the building. She didn't want to take any chances of a meeting putting her sister's life in jeopardy. The raid would be challenging enough with them entering into what was likely to be a heavily fortified situation.

"I'll have to bring in the feds." Bronson pulled out his phone and started to send a text, when Vincent's large hand clamped across the device.

"No feds. At least not until after. Sterling has a couple of agents in his pocket and they'll alert him to our operation. They'll destroy any files or documents tied to your brother's death. We need to keep the team small if we're going to find Aggie's sister. Then you can bring in anyone you want after that."

Aggie stood and moved toward the kitchen. "I'll call Ray." She looked back at Bronson for his approval. She knew he wasn't fond of her friend but what choice did they have? He gave her a nod and she scrolled through the numbers on her phone.

"Captain Ray Mitchell?" she heard Vincent ask him.

"The one and only," Bronson said. "Ray retired from the army about nine months ago. He has his own private security firm just north of Charlotte, North Carolina, not too far from Sterling. They're trained in tactical operations and have their own gear to help us."

"Yeah. I remember him. Where'd he get the money to set up his own private security outfit?"

"He said he's been working on it for years, using his savings to buy the land. He and his team have been effective, especially after we were attacked on his property."

"I'd be careful with him, Detective. Some people are not as they seem."

Aggie wasn't sure what Vincent meant by his statement. Ray had been the one to approve the operation to extract Vincent and his family from a dangerous situation in Afghanistan. If it hadn't been for the captain, Vincent would still be in the Middle East or maybe worse—dead.

Ray didn't pick up. Her call went to voicemail, but she didn't leave a message. Her longtime friend had never given her any reason not to trust him, but with Vincent interpreting most of the meetings, he'd have inside knowledge. She prayed he was wrong.

She tapped his number again. Still no answer.

Aggie stepped back into the living area. "Are you saying Ray's dirty?"

Vincent and Bronson both stared at her. "I was never able to pinpoint anything specific, but he always seemed to be around, listening and processing during every deal. He kept detailed reports of all of Sterling's meetings," Vincent said.

"Even the illegal ones?" Bronson asked.

"No, he never came to those, but there are ways to get around that."

"Did you get in touch with him?" Bronson asked.

Aggie shook her head. "Went to voicemail—and I didn't leave a message. I'll call him back later."

"Maybe we should head to the safe house

where we can talk in a more secure location."
Bronson motioned toward the bedroom. "I'll let
Ms. McDonald know we're leaving."

Vincent joined Aggie in the kitchen. Tonight
was the first time she'd seen the man since the
extraction. "I'm glad you and your family got
out safely."

"I suppose I have you and the army to thank
for that," he said. "How long did you say your
sister had been missing?"

She glanced at her watch. "Over forty-eight
hours."

"That's not good."

"Why do you say that?"

"From the research I've done and the meetings I've interpreted for Sterling Securities,
they never keep a hostage more than forty-
eight hours."

Strength faded from her body. She didn't
want to believe his words, but at the same time
she needed clarity. "What are you saying, Vincent?"

"I'm saying your sister is most likely dead."

ELEVEN

Ray's team, Oz, and a few elite SWAT team members filed into the large meeting room and took their seats at the rectangular tables equally spaced into five rows, two at each table. A metal podium stood at the front of the room and Bronson opened the blinds to the interior windows overlooking the bullpen.

After questioning Vincent Savoy last night, he'd put together an operation with his sergeant's approval and received permission to use Ray's team for a covert operation. A judge granted them a sealed search warrant and Bronson planned to lead the team inside Sterling's off-grid facility, tonight.

Outside the exterior windows of the room, Aggie covered her head from the light drizzle and ducked under the arm of an officer holding the main entrance door open. Today was the day he planned to bring her sister home.

A knock on the meeting room door announced

the arrival of Ray Mitchell. Vincent's warning replayed in Bronson's head but he'd vetted each one of them thoroughly and found nothing to keep Ray or any of his members from consulting. If he didn't need the man and his team's skills to get into Sterling, then he'd cut him loose, but since that wasn't the case, he'd just have to keep a close eye on their maneuvers.

"Grab a seat. We're about to start." Bronson motioned to the open table. Aggie entered behind Ray and took the adjacent seat, turning her body toward him in deep conversation. He overheard her sharing Vincent's revelation about her sister. If Aggie was planning something on the side, then he'd have to intervene.

When she glanced up at him, he motioned her to the front. "Hey, do you mind if we talk for a minute? In private?"

Aggie shot a quick look back in Ray's direction. "Sure."

He led her into the hallway away from others. "Listen, I know you're worried about Leslie and what we'll find today. I understand that what Vincent said last night has you spooked, but we've gone over every detail of this raid, and it's a solid plan."

She folded her arms across her chest. "I know."

"It just seems like after talking with Vincent last night, you've got more on your mind than the operation I've put together. Are you and Ray planning something outside of the scope of our raid?"

She shifted her weight to her other foot. "I'm going to do whatever it takes to find Leslie."

"And that's my plan, too."

"Yeah, but you're restricted by the confines of the search warrant to where you can go on the property. Ray's not."

It was a fair point—and part of the reason why they were working with Ray's team in the first place. "Remember what Vincent said about Ray. He's—"

"I heard him, but he's wrong. The man is clean, and he's got my back. Always has."

"And that's great as long as his support doesn't interfere or veer off course from the plan we have in place."

"We'll follow all of your instructions, but if we raid the facility and Leslie's not there, then that's a different story."

"You've cooked up an alternate plan?"

"Only if Leslie's not there."

Bronson glanced into the room and noticed Ray's stare. There was something about the man that got under his skin.

"You can't go off on your own, no matter what we find. I'm responsible for you and your safety. The only reason my sergeant gave

Ray's team permission to be part of this was because I promised no one would go rogue. Understood?"

She hesitated. "I'll do my best."

Oz walked toward them with a piece paper in his hand. "Aggie, can you give us a minute?"

With a nod, she returned to the room and her seat beside Ray.

Bronson watched them for a moment. "I don't like it."

"Don't like what?"

"Ray. He and Aggie are planning something if we don't find Leslie. I don't trust him."

"Then you're really not gonna like what I have to show you." Oz handed him the piece of paper and Bronson read to the middle of the page before looking up. "Are you kidding me?"

"I wish I was."

"Where did you find this?"

"In the unredacted documents we requested. Took me a while to get through them all but when I saw this, I wanted you to know."

"We're less than an hour from activation. I can't put together another team."

Oz looked into the room. "Question is, can you risk taking his team with you?"

Bronson looked back at the name listed in bold on the evidence paper. The serial number on the gun used in his brother's murder matched another military weapon issued to one Captain Ray Mitchell.

"Call the FBI and see if they will send an agent here. Fill them in on the details. This is their jurisdiction, and I can't arrest him, but I can delay."

Bronson strolled back into the room. He'd been right all along. Ray was guilty and now they had the evidence to prove it. All he needed to do was run the meeting long until an agent could arrive. There was no way he was taking the man who allegedly murdered his brother on their operation.

"Let's get this meeting started," Bronson said, keeping his eyes on Captain Mitchell.

Aggie stood outside the interrogation room door. Two federal agents had arrived at the precinct and taken Ray into a room for questioning. Minutes ticked by and the longer the delay, the more her anger festered. Ray couldn't have killed Corbin, but Bronson also wouldn't call in the feds without evidence. Her brain tumbled a million scenarios over in her mind, none of them making sense.

Bronson rounded the corner and Aggie pressed up from the wall. "Are they taking Ray into custody?"

"Not sure yet."

"I can't believe this."

Bronson handed her a piece of paper. "Then read the bolded print."

Aggie skimmed down to the middle of the page. The typed words chilled her anger.

"This must be a mistake." She looked back at Bronson. "There's no way Ray shot your brother. He'd die for his soldiers before he would take one of their lives. That's the kind of man he is."

"Sometimes men only let you see what they want you to see. You can't be sure what he did after he left your chopper."

"He was trying to survive and keep his men safe. As soon as I dropped his unit onto the roof, the nightmare erupted. I can promise you the only thing on his mind was securing the hostage and getting his team out of there alive."

She handed the paper back to him and crossed the hallway into the lounge for a quieter space to have their argument. Plus, she needed caffeine. Bronson followed her.

"Then why is his gun listed on the evidence report matching the one that killed my brother?"

There was half a pot left. She wondered how long it had been sitting there, but then again, she didn't care. Aggie grabbed a cup and poured. "There has to be an explanation. I'm telling you he didn't do this."

"Well, I need to know for sure."

"After all the years we were together, I thought the one thing we had was trust, but I clearly see that's gone, too."

She lifted her cup and moved back into the hallway outside the interrogation room when the agent in charge exited. He looked over her head at Bronson who emerged behind her. "I was coming to find you. Looks like he's innocent."

"But the round that killed Corbin Young came from his gun."

"Which was recorded as a battlefield loss."

"What does that mean?" Bronson asked.

"When a weapon is lost during the chaos of a mission, like Captain Mitchell's, then they record it as a battlefield loss. This is the case in his situation."

"He could've tossed it after he shot my brother and then claimed it as a battlefield loss."

"Except we have extended reports of the mission in question. Ray wasn't with your brother when he was shot. Corbin was separated from the group in the midst of the chaos. Ray was with the larger group of soldiers, and they all testified the same details regarding the operation."

Aggie's relief at the news mixed with her frustration toward Bronson. She'd tried to tell him Ray was innocent. "Great. So, he's cleared?"

The federal agent nodded. "There's no evidence to arrest him. So, yes, he's cleared. However, regarding what you've uncovered about Sterling Securities, we're going to need to take that with us."

Bronson nodded. "Of course. And the search for her sister?"

"ASAC Smith has agreed to let that continue but Agent Greene and I will be accompanying you. We'll lead the raid on Sterling and take any evidence back to the Bureau while your team hunts for the girl. I'll go grab my partner and we'll join the meeting."

Aggie was thankful they didn't stop the operation all together and hoped Leslie was still alive after all the delays. "Then we need to stop wasting everyone's time and get back to finding my sister." She straightened. "You think you can do that, Detective?"

Without waiting for his answer, she put her hand on the interrogation room handle to summon Ray back to the briefing.

"Wait," Bronson said. "As long as you promise not to do anything foolish once we're on Sterling's property. I couldn't take another loss like my brother's. Especially if it was you, Aggie."

She blinked at his revelation and willed herself to stay angry, but his concern resonated as genuine. Bronson's ultimate goal was to protect the ones he loved. He'd always been that way—with Corbin, with her sister and with her. How could she be frustrated with that?

Her anger faded. "Okay."

He nodded toward the door. "Then get your friend."

Aggie did as instructed and motioned for the captain to follow. "Time to fly."

Ray stood with a smile. "Fangs out."

"Fangs out."

She tapped his fist with hers, returned to the briefing room, and then made her way to the hangar with the rest of the team after the meeting ended.

Aggie scanned the late evening sky. The winds had kicked up around her and a low rumble thundered in the distance. She never liked flying at night, and the approaching storm clouds made her that much more uneasy. She'd have to readjust her plan a bit.

Ray's gaze followed hers. "Looks like we're flying through some nasty weather tonight. You okay with that?"

"I'll be fine. Just gotta kick the tires and light the fires."

"Sounds good. I'll see ya after preflight."

Aggie smiled and tried to push the news of Ray's stolen weapon to the back of her mind.

He'd never mentioned the theft to her. Military weapons did get stolen sometimes, but Ray was meticulous about all of his equipment. He double-checked every detail. Why didn't he tell her back when it happened?

She understood if he was embarrassed by the incident and wanted to keep it quiet, but they'd known each other for years. He was her father figure after her dad died and he even helped her through the breakup. Maybe their relationship was more one-sided than she thought.

Another crack of thunder rolled across the sky. She finished up her checklist and took her position.

The team loaded into the chopper, Ray with them in the back, while Bronson took the seat beside her.

"Ready?"

"Almost." She made a few adjustments and with permission for takeoff granted, she twisted the throttle, raised the collective lever with her left hand until the skids lifted off the ground. The Sterling Securities location they were targeting was due south. She pressed the cyclic control forward.

Drops of rain spattered and ran down the windshield the entire flight. Dark mountains loomed in the distance, and she lifted the helicopter a bit higher into the air, hoping to find a path without as much turbulence. Wind pressed against the fuselage, jostling the craft with vibrations. It wasn't pleasant, but she'd flown in worse. At least there were no explosions or guns firing at them. Aggie pressed forward.

"Lightning," Bronson said as another gust tipped them a bit to the left.

Aggie corrected and leveled the copter. "Noted. ETA ten minutes."

She kept her mind focused on the flight. A distracted pilot often made mistakes, resulting in a crashed aircraft or death. She didn't want to end up on a video streaming service as "what can go wrong" fodder for people's morbid curiosity. Her hands remained firmly in control as she battled the storm.

The drop-off point was a flat field about a mile away from the off-grid Sterling Securities complex. Far enough that the company's security radars would not pick up their landing but close enough to hike in under the cover of night.

The helicopter pitched to the right. A click and static filtered through the comms system. Bronson gripped the five-point harness holding him in his seat. "If the storm's too much, we can find another landing spot or delay the operation's timeline."

Aggie adjusted the throttles again and glanced

over. He looked pale. Not surprising after the last time they'd been in a helicopter. "All's well, Detective. Just a little storm. Nothing I haven't dealt with before."

The words were no sooner out of her mouth than the chopper tilted again, but instead of simply readjusting, the gust triggered a spin. Red lights flashed, dousing the cockpit in a crimson glow. Alarms drowned out the motor's familiar hum.

The chopper weaved and bobbed in the storm. Her left engine sputtered. Aggie worked quickly, but as she fought for control, seconds seemed to stretch into hours.

The storm shoved them in random directions, and she kept the fuselage from tipping forward. Mist and fog cloaked the surrounding terrain in darkness. There was no spot to land. Everything was steep, mountainous terrain.

Bronson pointed ahead. "Obstacle, Aggie."

She pulled the cyclic to the left in an effort to avoid a rock outcropping. The copter tilted, but they were too close. She scraped the stone slab and the chopper dove toward the ground.

TWELVE

Aggie fought for control. The hit had damaged the tail rotor and she had to set them down. They were still too far from their designated location and although a crash was unavoidable, if she could mitigate the landing, they might survive.

Bronson pointed to the GPS. "There. We can land in that field. We're only a couple of miles from Sterling. The hike will be a bit longer, but we can adapt."

"Ten-four. I hope I can stick the landing."

"I have no doubt."

She chose not to look at his face. Doubt often lived in a person's expression rather than in their words and she couldn't handle any skepticism. Not now.

Instead, she focused on her instrument panel, which was currently lit up like Times Square. "I'll have to do a running landing."

Ray leaned forward from the back. "That will cause a rollover."

"Not if I use the cyclic to stop all ground speed. I'll chop the throttle and use a normal hover to land."

"Like you did in Kabul?"

"Exactly."

Aggie maneuvered the chopper, fighting the spin caused by the damaged tail rotor and using the wind to counterbalance the engine torque. The landing wasn't smooth, but she was able to place the skids on the ground without toppling.

She flipped the switches and powered down the blades. Adrenaline rushed through her and into her trembling hands.

Bronson wrapped her chilled fingers in the warmth of his and squeezed. "Amazing."

The rest of the team erupted into cheers. As much as Aggie appreciated the praise, there was something more important calling for their attention—her sister.

"Thank you, but we've got a job to do. Let's find Leslie."

Bronson flipped the night vision goggles fastened to his helmet in front of his eyes and scanned the perimeter of the building.

The two agents led the teams to the outskirts of the property without any resistance from Sterling's men. So far, they seemed to be undetected, giving them the advantage of their surprise search and seizure. Any delay upon entry could give Sterling or his guards time to destroy evidence or kill Leslie.

The buildings before them rose into the air three stories high. A small yard encircled the entire campus, giving any guards placed on the roof a visual advantage.

Aggie shifted next to him and remained low under the coverage of the tree line. "There are at least twenty guards just on this one side. How are we going to move forward? We're outnumbered."

"We're going to stick to the plan—divide into two teams, we'll enter through the back and the federal agents will take our search warrant and walk through the front doors."

"You don't think a sneak attack would be better? You know, find a point and breach an unguarded entrance so we can get to my sister faster?"

"Once a door kicker, always a door kicker."

"I was a pilot not a door kicker, but I have to admit our units got the job done."

"Well, we aren't in Afghanistan anymore and Sterling will sue. This has to be by the book if the feds want the evidence to hold up in court."

She shifted beside him. "I don't care what happens in court. I care about Leslie."

"That's why we use two teams. Sneak attack from the back to find Leslie and distracting search and seizure at the front. You have to be patient and wait for their signal, then we'll go in through the back and find Leslie."

The agent's voice came through their comms devices and Bronson moved his team into place.

"Execute. Execute. Execute." The order came through.

Bronson, Aggie, and Oz, followed by Ray's team, moved in formation and aimed their weapons at the two guards standing at the back door.

"Police. Put your weapons down."

They obeyed, placing their AR-15s on the ground.

Bronson nodded toward the door. "Open it."

The taller guard tapped his badge to a box and the entrance clicked. The team entered, fanning out across the warehouse floor.

Palmer Sterling stormed down the metal steps at the side of the industrial space, his face red. "Detective, what are you doing?"

Bronson handed him a copy of the warrant. "Federal agents are onsite. This is a search and seizure. All of your computers, your hard drives, documents, anything that may be tied to weapons trafficking and the abduction of Leslie Newton will be confiscated."

"That's ridiculous. I've never been involved in weapons trafficking. Don't you think the government would drop my contract if that were the case? I would never take a risk like that."

"We have a witness and evidence that tells us otherwise."

Palmer continued blustering, but Bronson was happy to ignore him. "Take it up with the federal agents in the front of the building, Sterling. I'm just following their orders."

After an hour of searching every room, hallway, supply closet, and office space, Aggie walked up to him. "She's not here."

"Did you search every room?"

"The receptionist gave me the main key. Ray and I have searched every room and Leslie is not on the premises. Did they find out that we were coming?"

"We kept this tight. No way they knew."

"Remember what Vincent said about the feds. I keep wondering if they're on Sterling's payroll and gave him a heads up. If so, then they moved her. That's the only explanation."

"Unless they don't have her," Bronson said.

He hated to even entertain the idea but, so far, all the evidence the feds had collected revealed legitimate contracts and official business documents. They still had a long way to go but Bronson expected to find more by now. He expected to find Leslie.

Aggie exited the building. She needed some fresh air. Every room had been searched with nothing to hint her sister had ever been there.

A loud crack of thunder boomed around her and shook her nerves even more. She took cover under the overhang of the building. Lightning flashed across the field and rain poured, pounding the tin roof.

She lowered her night vision goggles over her eyes and scanned the campus before spotting a utility building off to the right at the back of the property. A white van drove out of a gravel drive and disappeared over the horizon, but the van wasn't what caught her attention.

Parked at the back, a gray truck sat underneath a streetlight. She had to get a closer look. Aggie jogged to the tree line, then through the woods. One guard stood at the front.

Aggie moved to the back of the building to avoid him. A metal door secured with a black box was her only way inside. Although these types of features usually indicated a locked position with a red light, this box's light was not lit. Perhaps it wasn't engaged.

She tried the handle. Locked.

"Time for Plan Fang," she said, then opened her backpack, rifled through and pulled out a set of picks she brought with her. She hoped the alternative plan she and Ray put together was enough to find her sister.

Aggie opened the door and propped the entrance with a rock. Security systems could be controlled from the inside, and she didn't want to take a chance on getting locked in with a murderer.

If Leslie was here, she would find her. Aggie prayed Palmer and his team were busy watching the commotion of officers raiding Sterling Securities' other facility, giving her the advantage of sneaking through the shadows. A scream echoed through the hallway. Aggie aimed her weapon and moved in that direction.

"Please don't. I have a daughter. Don't kill me."

Leslie.

Aggie moved toward the voices. Metal racks lined the entire building, leaving narrow aisles for her to maneuver. Wooden crates were stamped with the initials VS, burned into the lids and sides of the boxes. She lifted one not sealed. Dozens of schematics and drawings for semiautomatic weapons filled the inside and Sterling's logo had been replaced with the dominant VS. Each diagram was printed and would be almost impossible to track after they left the US but easy to sell to the highest bidder.

She kept moving, weaving in between the crates. The stench of gunpowder and gasoline fumes increased. Aggie stifled a cough and peered through the slats into the main room. Leslie sat in a chair, bound with ropes. Vincent stood with his back to Aggie, gun pointed at her head.

Forklifts sped around the pair, as if her sister's death wasn't imminent. The workers continued loading crate after crate into the vans. Once the vehicles were filled, they moved out, taking as many of the stolen diagrams with them as possible.

If only she could get to her. But Vincent would see her coming. Aggie needed a distraction.

She spotted a forklift parked at the back, and moved in that direction. The battery was charged, and she released the emergency brake, but she needed weight to place on the gas pedal. Several small crates lined the shelf next to her, along with a box cutter. She slipped the knife into her pocket, lifted the box, and placed the crate on the accelerator. The forklift sped forward, headed straight for the wall opposite her sister. Aggie raced back to her hiding place, a short distance away.

Within seconds, a loud crash rumbled through the building. Voices shouted. Men ran toward the commotion, including Vincent. Leslie was alone.

Aggie rushed forward, knife in hand and cut the ropes. "I'm gonna get you out of here."

"You found me. How?"

"No time for talking. Let's go before he comes back."

Her sister's eyes shifted and then widened. "Behind you."

The strike came hard and quick to Aggie's temple. She stumbled but pivoted, holding the knife out in front of her.

Vincent kept his gun aimed. "I don't think that's going to help you any, but I'm glad you showed up. You're going to be a big help to me in case your detective boyfriend arrives."

Aggie held her hands at her side and dropped the knife. His gaze followed the object to the floor, giving her a moment to retrieve her gun from its side holster. "I always bring a gun to a gun fight."

His lips curved into a sinister smile. He moved his arm and aimed at Leslie. "You might want to put that away or your sister gets a bullet between the eyes."

"And so will you." She took a couple of steps to move his direct line of sight away from Leslie even though his weapon remained aimed at her. "Maybe that would be best. The jail time you're going to get when the feds show up and confiscate all your stolen schematics will make you wish you were dead. You'll go away for the rest of your life. Nothing worse than trading your newly gained freedom for a ten-by-ten cell."

"I'm not afraid of dying, Aggie."

Sweat beaded on Vincent's forehead and Aggie noticed the dark spots on his hands and lower arms. Yellow discoloration tinged the whites of his eyes.

"Are you sick? You look a lot worse than the last time I saw you."

His eyes narrowed.

Black. Cold. No mercy.

He straightened, raised his arm at her sister and fired. The shot echoed through the building.

Bronson's feet pounded the ground as he ran toward the building at the back of the property. Only one shot had been fired and Aggie had gone missing.

Please God, let her be alive.

Several vans moved out a back road to the main highway. He radioed his team.

"Shots fired. All units to the back of the property."

Bronson, Oz, and Ray raced into the front of the warehouse building, their team behind them. Workers, surprised by the unit dressed in full tactical gear including semiautomatic weapons, stopped midstride. Fork truck operators turned off their vehicles and put their hands in the air.

"Everyone along that back wall. Move!" Bronson herded them all like the criminals they were, but Vincent wasn't among them.

A heavy back metal door slammed, and Bronson motioned for Oz, Ray, and two others to follow him. The rest of the team stayed with the workers.

They moved through the aisleways stacked with crates of stolen schematics and advanced toward the middle of the building.

A lone chair sat in the open square with cut ropes lying on the floor. Leslie nor Aggie were in sight, but a smear of blood lined the concrete and faded into the darkness of the back aisles.

Bronson signaled for the others to continue through the stacks, clearing each path to the rear of the building. More blood directed their direction.

He wondered if it was Aggie's or Leslie's. He figured they were both alive since they hadn't come across a body yet and he prayed they didn't.

They reached the back exit and Bronson signaled for Oz to breach the door, but something was on the other side. They shoved until the barrier gave way. Bronson stepped out ready for an attack.

Instead, he found Leslie unconscious and bleeding from a bullet wound to her leg. She let out a moan when he pressed his fingers to her neck.

"Hang in there, Leslie," Bronson said, and tightened a cord one of the other officers found inside, around her leg as a tourniquet.

Oz radioed for an ambulance, then straightened to scan the area with night vision.

"Bronson. Two o'clock."

He stood and looked through his goggles to the area Oz indicated. Two people moved along the perimeter of the overgrown field. One was Aggie. The other, was Vincent Savoy.

Sirens echoed through the air and cruisers, with their blue lights blazing, pulled up in front of the building, but Aggie had no way of alerting them to her position, already hidden in the thick underbrush. She prayed they found Leslie. Vincent knocked her sister unconscious at the exit to keep her from slowing them down due to her wounded leg. At least, she was still alive.

The metal barrel of his weapon pressed into her back. "Pick up the pace."

She moved forward through the thick underbrush. Thorns scratched her arms and pant legs. Rain poured on top of them, making the trek challenging. Her vision doubled, and her head ached from the earlier hit Vincent induced with the grip of his gun. She struggled to move forward.

The fierce ringing in her head muffled his words. Her eyesight blurred from her injuries and darkness closed the periphery of her vision. She stumbled to the ground. Vincent grabbed her arm and jerked her back to her feet. "Don't make me shoot you."

The two-mile hike back to the chopper drained what little strength she had left in her legs. She needed a plan. With the helicopter's damaged tail rotor, there was no way they'd complete the flight to Charlotte and the blow to her head had taken its toll. Maybe she could use that to her advantage.

A wave of weakness surged through her, and she stumbled again but remained upright. Pain shot through her head and her stomach rolled. If she could hang on until Bronson and the team reached them, maybe she'd live through this nightmare.

"I don't think I can fly," she said.

"Nice try." He pressed the gun into her back again.

"My vision's impaired and I have symptoms of a concussion. If I fly, we'll crash."

"Then I guess we'll both die."

She had to convince him to leave her behind and take the chopper himself. He wouldn't need a hostage if she convinced him he could fly the craft on his own and escape the police.

"You can fly the helicopter. You'd have a better outcome than me trying to fly almost blind."

"I doubt that."

The trees cleared and the chopper came into view. A crash of thunder vibrated the ground around them, and the downpour intensified. She tried again. "I can't fly in this weather."

"This storm's not any worse than the night you flew your troops into my village and took out my brother's house."

She slowed her steps, trying to remember the mission he mentioned. "What are you talking about?"

"My family and I had just left from a dinner with my oldest brother, his wife, and daughter. He and his other guests didn't make it out alive because rockets were launched from your helicopter, killing them all."

"Different pilots fly different missions. I doubt that was mine."

"I don't get my details mixed up. Tail number 737. May the third. Two years ago. You were listed as the pilot. I interpreted the records for the Afghan Army."

Aggie remembered the mission. The man harbored terrorists in his home who used women and children as human shields. He'd been the mastermind behind many of the terrorist attacks around the globe. Gunners took out the immediate threat when they flew over the compound. They would have stopped with the initial attack, but the man's wife picked up a rocket launcher and aimed it toward the helicopter. They eliminated her, too. The sadness of the story remained with Aggie.

Vincent opened the door and shoved her inside the fuselage, then joined her on the passenger side. Sweat, body odor, and a rancid stench entered with him.

Nausea rolled within her. She tried to focus on the instruments. "The panel is dim. Turn on the flashlight so I can see."

"The flashlight's on."

Despite the glow from his phone, Aggie fumbled and flipped switches, not sure if they were the correct ones to start the chopper.

"I can't see it. My vision is getting worse." She leaned her head back against the seat and closed her eyes. She must have a bleed probably pressing on her optic nerve. If his hit had induced a slow hemorrhage in her brain, then she'd need immediate medical care which wasn't coming anytime soon.

With all of her deployments and close calls, she'd planned, even trained, for the end of her days, but now that death stared her in the face, the one person she wanted by her side was Bronson. Only the hand of God could save her now.

A metal barrel pressed against her temple, bringing her thoughts back to the present. "Start her up."

"I'm telling you, something's wrong. I can barely see the instrument panels."

He pressed harder. "Then use what vision you have and your muscle memory to get this bird in the air. Then I'll take over and you can land."

"Unless I'm dead by then."

"I barely hit you."

"I'm pretty sure I have a brain bleed thanks to that hit, so you better start brushing up on any flying skills you may have learned in the army."

He grabbed her chin and directed her face to his. He flashed the light into her eyes, then released her.

"My pupils aren't equal, are they?"

He ignored her question. "Get her started."

"You know I'm not lying. You don't want me

to fly." Aggie slid her hands across the controls, trying to make out each one. She activated the start sequence.

Blades whirred to life above her and the rhythmic sound of the engine hummed. This was the moment she usually lifted from the ground but with a broken tail rotor, as soon as she did, the chopper would rotate into a spin and Vincent would know his only escape was a death trap.

"I think I'm gonna be sick." She placed a hand over her mouth and reached for the door handle.

With a click, cool air rushed inside. His hands gripped her shoulders and with a shove, she fell out the door. Her body thudded against the damp ground, while dust and debris peppered her face. She covered her head with her arms and raised a prayer of thanks to God who provided protection when she needed Him most.

"Don't try to find me or I'll hunt you down and kill you and your family," he shouted, then slammed the pilot door closed.

With Vincent's final words, the force of the down draft washed across her as the chopper rose. Another gunshot split the air. Aggie's pain faded into black.

THIRTEEN

Bronson moved through the thick brush and followed the blood trail either left by Aggie or Vincent. He hoped it was from the latter.

They were headed back in the direction of the chopper, but with the aircraft having a busted tail rotor, any flight would be almost impossible. He had to stop Vincent before they took off.

The wind picked up and the familiar chop of helicopter blades filtered through the air.

He was too late.

Gunshots fired and Bronson sprinted in the direction of the sound.

A call reported through the radio. "Shots fired. Shots fired. Suspect fleeing the scene. Male, black hoodie, approximately two hundred and fifty pounds. Officer returned fire but unable to stop the suspect. He's in possession of a helicopter."

Bronson tore through the trees and thickets

until he reached the extraction point. The helicopter blades were in full motion when he breached the tree line but the chopper was too far into the sky for him to see if Aggie was inside.

The craft weaved and bobbed in the air. Without the tail rotor operating, she'd have to fight to keep them from descending into a full-blown death spin.

Ray and Oz caught up to Bronson. The helicopter swept across the field, then tipped back in the opposite direction.

"She's on the ground." Ray pointed to their right. Bronson followed his gaze and scanned the area, through the grass. Aggie faced away from them, on her side, not moving.

She wasn't in the air and for that he was thankful. He raced over and rolled her onto her back—unconscious, a faint pulse and blood covering the side of her face. He turned on his flashlight and directed the bright beam into her eyes.

"Her pupils are unresponsive."

Oz clicked his radio. "We need an ambulance at the extraction point."

The call response came back. "We don't have a road to you, but we confiscated an all-terrain vehicle. Sending paramedics along the east side of the tree line."

Aggie stirred and Bronson held her hand. "I'm here, Aggie. We've got you."

He looked up at Vincent still battling with the chopper. "We've got to get out of here before he crashes that thing on top of us," he said as he lifted Aggie into his arms. He started for the tree line, keeping his eye on the sky.

Vincent rose higher into the air. The helicopter continued to pitch and bob back and forth across the field. The man swept low and dug one of the skids into the ground. The fuselage tipped forward, onto its nose, and the chopper flipped several times. Blades shattered into shrapnel and then the craft stilled.

Oz radioed for SWAT officers to advance, but before they could take a step, fire exploded into the sky, enveloping them in a wave of heat. The force pushed Bronson to the ground. He covered Aggie's body with his own and prayed for God's protection, one more time.

Alarms beeped and low voices whispered Aggie awake. Bright lights glared into her eyes, and she quickly closed them again, taking in a deep breath. Muted tones of spiced cologne overladen with the strong scent of Italian food permeated the room.

Bronson. And... Sal's?

His fingers pressed against her palm and

lifted her hand to his lips. The kiss warmed her soul. He didn't leave her. Not this time.

"Aggie, you're in the hospital but I'm here."

She squeezed his hand back and licked her lips. He placed a cool ice chip against her mouth for her to take. The refreshing temperature helped wet her tongue. "Leslie?"

"She's fine. She went to pick up Holly and said they'd be back in a little while for a visit. Your mom stepped outside to make some phone calls. A lot of Mills Creek townspeople want to know how you're doing, and Sal sent you some of his lasagna."

"I thought I smelled his cooking." She squinted at him. "Can you cut the lights?"

He released her hand for a moment and the chair scraped across the tile floors, then the glare was gone.

"Is that better?" His hand was back in hers.

She opened her eyes and saw his face. His features were blurry, but she was so thankful he was by her side. "Much," she said. "Thank you."

He lifted her fingers and kissed them again. "I'm so glad you're okay."

"Where's Vincent?"

"Dead. He crashed the helicopter. With the busted tail rotor, his lack of pilot experience, and the storm, he drove the bird into the ground and then the chopper exploded."

"That makes two helicopters Ray's lost within a few days. The insurance company's not going to like that. I imagine he's not happy, either."

"He mumbled a few choice words when he saw the debris."

She bit back a laugh. "I guess he won't be needing me to fly for him after all."

Bronson's worried expression softened a bit. Humor always helped deflate tense situations between them, burying the words that really needed to be said.

His thumb brushed across her knuckles several times. Like he was nervous about something.

"What's up?"

"I don't know what I would've done without you. I saw you lying there in the field, and I thought he killed you. Just like he killed my brother. I don't ever want to feel—"

His voice cracked with emotion, and she squeezed his hand. "I'm going to be fine. It's just a little bump on the head. I've dealt with far worse when I was in the military."

Bronson cleared his throat. "The doctor told your mom and Leslie that you have a small subdural hematoma that is regressing, and you should make a full recovery. He's worried about your vision since the bleed pressed on your optic nerve. Are you able to see me okay?"

His blurry figure was more than okay. "There's three of you—which isn't necessarily a bad thing—but I'm sure that will get better with time."

"He said that was normal, but he wants to keep you overnight for observation as a precaution. Do you remember Vincent hitting you in the head?"

Pieces of the trauma flashed into her mind. "I remember going into the warehouse and seeing my sister tied to the chair. I went to cut her loose and then Vincent attacked. She's okay, right? I remember him shooting her in the leg."

"It ended up only being a flesh wound. They cleaned and dressed it, then released her. She's got a limp, but nothing was going to stop her from getting to Holly."

Aggie inclined the hospital bed a bit more and took a sip from the water jug on the side table. "What about Vincent's wife and daughter? Are they okay?"

"Federal agents have the case now, but they did tell us that Vincent's wife was poisoning him with arsenic. She confessed when they questioned her based off the medical examiner's report."

"That's why he looked so sick when I saw him last. Why did she poison him?"

"She said he brought dishonor to their family name and placed their daughter in danger. She hated him for betraying them and decided if she had the money then she and her daughter could live in peace. The feds took her into custody and placed the girl into witness protection with her aunt who agreed to enter the program, too."

"How horrible for that little girl. Her father's dead and now she's lost her mother, too."

He frowned. "Sounds like she might be better off without them."

Exhaustion consumed her and Aggie nodded but struggled to stay awake.

"Before you go to sleep," Bronson leaned forward, and she forced her eyes half open again. "There's something I need to say. I've waited long enough."

He paused.

"I've always loved you, Aggie. I don't think I ever stopped. Ending our relationship was the dumbest thing I've ever done. The grief from my brother's death did a number on me. The anger rooted in me, and I pushed everybody away, but I promise I won't ever do that again. Will you forgive me and give me another chance?"

His words stirred her soul. She never thought she'd hear him apologize. He'd broken her heart, leaving her in pieces. In some ways, her decision to leave the army stemmed from losing him. She tried to think of the right thing to say but struggled to process her feelings. The meds dripping into her veins and clouding her judgement didn't help.

"I forgave you a long time ago, Bronson. There's no need to rehash everything."

"Then we can start over?"

Hope resonated in his voice. She hated to disappoint him, but the hurt he caused still lived in her memory, fresh and raw. Getting over Detective Bronson Young was the hardest thing she'd faced. Harder than dodging bullets and flying Black Hawks into combat zones.

"I need some time. A lot has happened—from Corbin's death to my sister's abduction. I want to be with my family, play with Holly and most of all, rest in Jesus. I can't make any commitments right now."

He dropped his gaze to their hands still clasped together. "I understand."

The alarm on her IV monitor began to beep, indicating low fluid. He released her hand, stood, and hit the quiet button. "The nurse will be here in a minute to change it out for you. I guess I better go."

She touched his arm. "Before you do, tell me what happened with Palmer Sterling? Was he involved in the abduction?"

"Not that we could find. Our team combed through all the financial documents from our search and there weren't any money trails tying Palmer to Leslie's kidnapping or weapons trafficking."

"What about the building? Wasn't that Sterling's property?"

"Palmer said he leased the building through a property management company and other than signing the contract or seeing his rental income in his bank account, he really didn't know much about the occupants. He said the property management company ran background checks and vetted all leases, but apparently someone didn't perform their due diligence and he'd be taking a more active role in future rentals. All the evidence backed up his story."

"He never saw the vans going in and out of the property?"

Bronson lifted his jacket from the back of the chair. "He said he spent most of his time at the main headquarters and even when he did go to the off-grid facility, he assumed they were shipping their products like most businesses do."

Heels clicked on the tile floor and Leslie entered the room with Holly by her side. "You're awake." They stopped just inside the door. "Did we interrupt something? Should we come back later?"

"Absolutely not." Aggie reached for her niece. "I want to see my Holly bug. Put her right here on my bed."

Leslie sat her daughter on the mattress for a good auntie hug and took a seat in a chair. Holly looked up at Bronson, moving toward the door. "Thank you for finding my mommy."

He placed a hand on her head and ruffled her curls. "You need to be thanking your aunt Aggie for that one. She's the one who found your mother." Bronson looked at Aggie and gave her a sad smile. "I'm gonna go. I've got some paperwork to finish at the office."

"Maybe we can catch up in a few days, after they release me."

"I'd like that." He bent forward, close to Aggie's ear. "I'm not giving up on us. Not again."

The warmth of his kiss touched her cheek, and he squeezed her fingers, leaving her with a complicated decision to consider.

A week after Aggie was discharged, Bronson headed into the precinct dreading the continued mountain of paperwork he was still combing through regarding the case. The joint effort with the federal agents didn't make the reports any easier.

At least Aggie was at home now. She had a few lingering effects with her vision, but the neurologist said those symptoms should improve as her body reabsorbed the bleed. Bronson prayed her vision returned to normal so she could fly again. Such talent didn't deserve to be sidelined forever. Even if she only flew for fun, that was better than nothing.

He planned to visit the farm but wanted to give her plenty of time to think about their relationship. He loved her, always had, and he was ready to move forward with a fresh start. He hoped Aggie would choose the same.

He didn't blame her for being wary. He was scared, too, but God had given him peace about not giving up hope. Maybe a few of her favorite flowers would be a nice surprise when he stopped by after work.

Bronson pressed open the bullpen door and walked to his desk situated opposite from Oz. His partner stood across the room, talking to the new female detective. She was single, gorgeous, and seemed to have taken an interest in his partner.

Bronson made his way into the break room and poured a cup of black coffee. He really needed the entire pot to keep him awake since he planned to stare at a computer screen for the next ten hours. After a couple of sips, he walked back to his desk and Oz joined him, his own mug in hand.

"Glad to see you're done flirting."

His partner leaned back in his chair and lifted his mug for a sip. "Just wanted to make her feel welcome. She's nice."

"What's her name again?"

"Eliza Burke. She's working with the narcotics division."

"So, you *can* date her."

Oz twisted his chair back around for another glance in the woman's direction. "Technically, yes, but you know me. I'm not one to date cops."

"Yeah. Okay. Unlike the last two women you took out."

"And those two proved my theory as to why I don't date cops," he said, facing forward again.

Bronson sat down. "As long as she doesn't distract you from finishing these reports we've been chipping away at all week. If I didn't know any better, I would think the thing multiplied overnight."

He placed a hand on several paper files and documents. "I'll be glad when we can put this one fully behind us."

"Not sure that's going to happen." Oz wheeled his chair around to the side of Bronson's desk. "FBI sent this to me this morning."

Oz tapped his screen and let a video play.

"This is a clip agents found from the Sterling Securities raid. Apparently, Sterling had all his employees wear body cameras during their ops. Since Vincent interpreted for Sterling, he wore one. They were supposed to keep them running all the time, but Vincent picked his recording sessions. However, he did turn his camera on the night he was extracted. It recorded everything."

Bronson turned the phone to enlarge the video but couldn't determine the identity of the man with Vincent. "That's not Corbin. Who is that?"

"I had our cybersecurity team clean up the images and compare what we had with all the employee and contractor photos from Sterling. Vincent's partner that night was Lee Demsky."

Oz swiped to the next clip. "Here he is holding Corbin at gunpoint. Vincent's standing next to your brother, unarmed."

Bronson picked up a foam stress ball and squeezed. "Then Lee killed my brother? Not Vincent?"

"Correct. There's more."

Oz played another section of video from a different point of view on the camera. Lee, Corbin and Vincent ran towards the helicopter, with the latter recording the entire scene. Gunfire and IEDs exploded around them.

In the midst of chaos, Lee raised his arm,

aimed the weapon, and shot past Vincent, hitting Corbin. His brother fell to the ground. Aggie slammed her open palm against the window, eyes wide, staring at his brother's body. She turned, mouthed something to the other soldiers, who jumped from the back and lifted him inside.

Lee turned his narrowed gaze to her, then climbed through the door. The man fired, Corbin was hit, and Aggie was an eyewitness. Bronson turned his back to the phone. A flush of heat and grief coursed through him. He thought Corbin's killer had been brought to justice, but Lee was still walking around a free man.

"Does Lee know this video exists?"

"Shouldn't. This clip wasn't on the USB. I just got it this morning from the Bureau."

"But Lee worked for Palmer. Would he have seen it there?"

"Doubt it. Human resource documentation confirms they cancelled Lee's contract with the company at least a year before. However, when we looked into their security footage, Lee still had access to the building."

Bronson pushed from his desk and tossed the ball to Oz, who tossed it back—a game they played when they were trying to put the puzzle pieces of a case together. "How'd he manage that?"

"They found large deposits to one of Sterling's human resource assistants. A young college girl who created badges as part of her job and gave access whenever Lee wanted."

"Wonder if she knows she's an accessory to murder and weapons trafficking?"

"If she doesn't yet, I'm sure the FBI will tell her," Oz rolled his chair back to his desk and clicked his mouse a couple of times. "Get this. The night Corbin was killed, they were in the middle of a weapons deal. Maybe Corbin interrupted, saw what he wasn't supposed to see, and Lee took him out before he could report his activity. Make the shooting look like an accident in the middle of all the chaos."

The man was still at large. The case Bronson thought ended with the death of Vincent was not over.

"There's only one thing I don't get, why drop the USB on the chopper that night?" Oz tossed the ball back to Bronson, his turn.

He squeezed the foam in his hand. "Because Vincent was already planning to rat out Lee and take over the entire illegal billion-dollar operation. Lee wasn't trying to kill my brother. He was trying to kill Vincent and Corbin got hit instead."

"Then Lee came after Aggie because she had the USB."

"Does the FBI have him in custody now?"

"Not yet. The FBI requested our officers help canvas the area but after checking security cameras, cell phone towers and every digital footprint imaginable, we haven't been able to find him." Oz took a sip of his coffee. "But why would he stay around here?"

Bronson dropped the ball and dread knotted in his chest. "Because he thinks Aggie saw him pull the trigger."

FOURTEEN

The warm afternoon beckoned Aggie to the porch swing with a glass of apple cider. Rows of trees stretched across her family's acreage and the babble of the creek nearby relaxed her. She loved the hustle and bustle of workers as they tended their farm, the distant hum of equipment rousing memories of her father. She breathed in the fresh spring air and leaned back on a pillow, closing her eyes.

Her head injury was improving but she still needed extra rest for the next few weeks to give her brain time to heal. As an added complication, even though the man who caused her trauma, Vincent Savoy, was dead, the entire ordeal had triggered a bit of posttraumatic stress that put more strain on her injury. Her neurologist prescribed at least two months of rehabilitation.

She was thankful Vincent could no longer hurt her family, but his daughter having to enter witness protection continued to plague her thoughts. The poor girl must be devastated to lose both her parents in a matter of days. Why did so many people think more money would save their family when history proved the opposite?

Gravel crunched behind her and she sat up, her vision still a bit hindered. A black Cadillac sedan pulled into her driveway and a man emerged, wearing a ball cap pulled down over his eyes, jeans, and a polo shirt. A bouquet of tulips covered his face. Something about him seemed familiar as he walked up the steps.

"Bronson, is that you?"

"Now, I'm officially offended." Lee Demsky lowered the flowers for her to take. "Don't you know an old friend when you see him?"

"Lee? What are you doing here?" She rose, took the flowers, and gave him a hug.

"I heard you've had a rough go of life lately and I wanted to come by and check on you."

"Thank you. It's been forever." She took the flowers from him, and he leaned back against one of the posts. "Are you still working for Sterling?"

"I've gone a bit more freelance and contract with a couple of security firms. I like being able to choose which projects I do."

"I understand that." Aggie fingered one of

the tulip bulbs. "Well, welcome to Newton Apple Farm."

Lee turned his back to her and scanned the vast acreage of rolling hills and rows of trees. "You always said this place was stunning. I'm glad I came to see it for myself. You didn't exaggerate. Your home is gorgeous. Much like the lady."

Heat flushed her cheeks. "It's my happy place."

"How many acres does your family own?" He returned his gaze to her.

"A hundred and we're surrounded on three sides by national forest land. No one can ever build or develop next to us."

"A true safe haven."

"That, it is. Thanks so much for the flowers. They're beautiful, but surely you didn't come all this way just to bring me a get-well bouquet."

The corners of his lips curled into a smile. "I do have a bit of an ulterior motive."

"I figured. What's up?"

"I heard you left the army, and it surprised me. The last time we spoke, you said you wanted to have a lifelong career with the military. What changed?"

She eyed him for a moment, not sure what to make of his surprise visit and inquisition. Lee had taught her a few things about surveillance when they were in Afghanistan, but she never thought of him as a close friend. Not like Ray.

Something about his impromptu trip nagged her gut. "I wanted to reconnect with my family. I realized how much I missed being home and after ten years of service, the time to leave seemed as good as any."

He pressed up from the post he'd been leaning against and took a seat in one of the rockers. "I thought maybe it had something to do with that mission in Afghanistan, the one where we extracted the translator. As I recall, you were pretty shook up over the soldier's death."

"He was from my hometown—a friend of our family. Of course, I was upset."

He folded his arms across his chest. "Do you know what happened to him?"

Her heart rate increased. Something about his demeanor shook her to the core. She kept her answer vague. "Only what the army reported. He was shot."

"And that's it? That's all you know?"

His continued questions did little to ease her mind. He knew Vincent, worked for Sterling and was in Afghanistan. Three things that didn't seem like a problem after the closure of the case, until now.

"Tell you what." She forced a smile to her

face. "Let me put these in some water and then we can talk. Would you like some apple cider or sweet tea? My momma makes the best in the state."

She didn't wait for his answer but moved through the screen door into the kitchen. Maybe she was being paranoid. After all she'd been through with Vincent, a bit of wariness was expected.

Lee had always been nice to her and there was nothing in the case that implicated him.

"Is she here? I'd love to meet her," he said, while remaining on the porch.

"She's around."

She didn't need to let him know she was at the house alone. Aggie moved into the kitchen, found a vase, and added water for the buds. She lowered her nose into the pink tulips and inhaled.

These were the same flowers she received after Leslie's abduction. The card had been signed by Sterling Securities. Aggie stared at them a moment longer, the hairs on her neck rising.

The screen door creaked open behind her. Lee's footsteps thumped against the hardwood floors. Aggie straightened. All the pieces of the puzzle collided into one large, scary picture.

"You remember now, don't you?" he asked.

Flashes of the night Corbin died returned. Lee had been the last one on the chopper. From her line of sight, he came from the exact trajectory as the gunfire that had struck down Corbin.

Her weapon was upstairs in her bedroom. She gripped the crystal vase in her hand, then faced him. No running for her. She was a fighter and Lee knew she had skills from their military time together.

His voice held a sinister tone, similar to Vincent's when he was desperate to escape and had no problem harming anyone who got in his way. Funny how desperation fed their motive to kill.

"We can do this the easy or hard way," he said. "With your head injury, it might be best if you take too many of these pain pills I brought or you can choose the hard way and try to fight me, but you'll lose."

He held up an amber bottle of oxycodone and gave it a little shake. "The choice is yours."

Even on her best day, he'd be hard to combat and without being in peak condition, her chances of beating him were low, especially without her weapon. She'd have to physically fight him and after the damage Vincent did, she was far from the top of her game.

Aggie launched the vase at his head and

sprinted onto the back porch. Mac rose to his feet at the commotion as she fled from the house.

The sound of glass shattered behind her, and booted steps pounded.

"Mac, Attack." The command ignited her dog into action.

He lunged when Lee exited the door, giving Aggie time to run to the barn. Her head pounded with the exertion and her lungs burned with every inhale. She willed her legs to move faster but the last few days of rest didn't help with her escape.

She looked back over her shoulder. Mac had his teeth gripped onto the man's leg, slowing Lee down, but not stopping him.

She was almost there and pushed herself up the small hill. The latch was stubborn, and Lee gained ground after freeing himself from her dog. She pulled on the latch again, but the door wouldn't budge.

"So much for your hiding place," he said, drawing closer.

Aggie fled around the side of the barn. Large tractors and equipment lined the building, but all of the workers were in the field. She looked for anyone to help her. No one was there.

His gun clicked behind her. "I would stop if I were you."

Aggie slowed her steps and turned. Lee Demsky walked toward her, gun raised at her head.

Bronson wheeled into the Newton farm driveway, slinging dust and gravel behind him. He'd left Oz at the station to organize a team. They'd arrive within a few minutes.

Mac stood, barking near the barn, and Bronson raced up the hill to the door. Voices from around the corner redirected his steps. He kept his weapon aimed as he stepped into position. Aggie stood with her hands in the air, backing away from Demsky. Open stalls with farm equipment and tractors were parked on her right.

"Demsky. Drop your weapon," Bronson said, as he walked closer.

The man halted and turned to the side, keeping his aim on Aggie. "Not gonna happen, Detective."

"Backup's on the way. You can't win this, Lee. Let me take you in without another body to add to the count. We know you killed Corbin."

Lee looked back to Aggie and sneered. "You can't prove it, if she's dead."

He fired his gun without hesitation, but Aggie lunged for cover, dodging the shot. Bronson pulled his trigger, striking Lee in the chest, but the wound barely fazed the man. Lee pulled up his shirt. "Kevlar, Detective. I'm no idiot."

Lee fired another round, hitting Bronson in the abdomen. Fiery pain pierced through him, and he dropped to the ground.

The sun glared in his eyes. He tried to move, but all his strength faded from his body. The last thing he saw was the black, faceless shadow walking towards the barn stall where Aggie took cover.

Tears pooled in Aggie's eyes, and she ducked lower behind her father's old farm truck, grabbing her phone to dial 911, but she had no service. If she didn't get to Bronson or get him help, he'd bleed out. She couldn't lose him. Not again.

Aggie raised up and peered through a dirty side window at the end of the stall, her vision still a bit blurry. Tractors rolled through the orchard toward the barn. The workers must've heard the shots. If she didn't act fast, then someone else might get hurt, but they also provided a distraction so she could get to Bronson.

Using the truck as a shield, Aggie crouched beside the front tire and peeked around the fender. Bronson tried to get up, but blood soaked the side of his shirt and he collapsed to the ground again. His weapon had fallen out of reach.

Lee walked through the stalls looking for her. "You're the last witness. If you come out, then I won't put a bullet in your boyfriend."

Lee opened the barn's side door and disappeared into the interior. Aggie used the moment to grab her father's shotgun from the back of his old truck. She couldn't risk running to Bronson without protection in case Lee returned and killed them both.

She checked the chamber, but the weapon was empty. Her father always kept ammunition in his truck somewhere. Aggie searched the floor and under the seat, then flipped open the glove compartment, to find a box with two buckshot rounds inside. Perfect for her impaired vision. As long as she was close, the ammo would find her target. She loaded the weapon and then crept to Bronson's side, keeping the shotgun within reach.

"We've got to get you out of here," she said and pressed a hand over his wound.

His gaze shifted to hers. "Can't."

"Yes, you can." Aggie lifted Bronson's arm around her shoulder and pulled him a few inches back toward the truck. He moaned in pain.

"If we can get to dad's truck then—"

An engine cranked in the stall next to them. Lee had exited the barn. He shifted the tractor into drive and lowered the forks. The wheels steered toward them both.

Aggie grabbed the shotgun. There was no time to waste. Her vision blurred a bit, but she aimed at the clearest target and fired both rounds.

Lee's body slumped forward across the steering wheel and turned the tractor into a tree.

Adrenaline rushed through her, trembling her body but Bronson needed her now. He'd lost too much blood and his face was pale.

"You saved me…again," he whispered.

She pressed her forehead to his. Relief flooded through her that he was still conscious. Maybe the wound wasn't as bad as she'd thought. "You think you'd learn after the first time."

Tractors drew closer and sirens sounded in the distance. One of the workers must've radioed for help. Aggie was tired of holding back. She pressed her lips to his, thanking God he was alive.

FIFTEEN

Two weeks later, Aggie walked through the rows of the apple orchard, keeping to the shade of the trees, and letting the breeze cool her from the late afternoon sun. Her vision was back to normal, and the doctor cleared her to start work, upgrading her family's security system. Not that they needed much now with Lee and Vincent both deceased.

"Hey, wait up," a male voice said from behind her.

Aggie turned, tipping up the brim of her old cowboy hat for a better view. Bronson looked more handsome than ever in his blue jeans and gray T-shirt, accentuating his toned physique. He used a cane to help him walk after his injury, adding a bit of sophistication to his allure.

A gentle breeze blew his sandy waves of blond hair back from his bright blue eyes. In his hand was a folder and a bouquet of white daisies.

"Hi there, stranger. I didn't know you were coming by," she said.

"Hard to reach you when you don't carry your phone to work."

She'd been to see him every day in the hospital after his surgery but had given him a break once they released him into his mother's care. The days apart had given them both time to think about their relationship.

"Yeah. I'm trying to enjoy the real-life beauty God's placed around me lately. Something almost dying taught me."

"I understand." He held out the bouquet of flowers when he reached her. "I hope it's okay I stopped by without calling first. I thought you might like these better than tulips."

She pressed her nose into the flowers and inhaled. "I'm supposed to be the one giving you flowers since you're the one wounded."

"I'm not really a flower kind of guy. Besides, you and your family kept me stocked in food while I was on the mend. I think a few flowers are the least I can do in return."

"I guess it *is* time I choose a new favorite flower. The white daises are perfect. Thank you."

She motioned toward the tractor parked one row over. "Wanna go for a ride?"

"Can we both fit in there?"

"I think I can make room."

She climbed into the air-conditioned cabin and patted the seat next to her. He handed her his cane and then gently pulled himself up. She started the tractor and steered them down to the edge of the creek bank, letting the hum of the machine fill the silence.

Bronson seemed content to let the quiet linger between them, too, even though there were so many things that needed to be said. Words escaped her in moments like these. She wasn't even sure how to say thank you for saving her sister's life and her own. Mere words of gratitude didn't contain enough depth for what was in her heart.

Aggie pulled into her favorite spot, cut the engine, and opened her door, while remaining in her seat. Water babbled across the rocks, butterflies flitted from one wildflower to another, and the scent of honeysuckle filled the cabin. Layered mountains stood in the distance as the sun sank behind them, coloring the sky with pink streaks.

"I brought you something else." Bronson handed her the folder.

She took the file and flipped open the cover. A black-and-white surveillance photo sat on top of several pictures. Aggie sifted through them. A young girl was at the park, playing on the swing set. Another showed her eating ice cream with a beautiful dark-haired woman.

"Vincent's daughter and is that her aunt? I thought they were in witness protection, and I know those guys would never let you have photos of them."

"The FBI cleared them of all threats, and they were able to exit the program to live their lives without fear. They found a nice neighborhood about an hour outside of Mills Creek. The aunt sends her gratitude."

"They don't hate me?"

"Of course not. Why would you ask that?"

"I'm the reason Vincent is dead. They might not have known what kind of man he was, but he was still the girl's father."

"Vincent chose his own path. He agreed to sell illegal military documents and tried to kill you and your sister. They know what kind of man he was and are grateful to the ones who saved them from the horror."

"You told them what he did?"

"Not knowing the truth about the death of a family member is the hardest thing for any person to handle. By giving them the full story, they can find closure and move forward. That's why I wanted you to have these photos. I want you to move forward, too…with me."

Aggie was at a loss for words. His kindness

was overwhelming. They both had struggled with his brother's death and the strain ended their relationship, but these photos were a true gift.

"Check the back." Bronson flipped the image over and read a Bible verse he'd written.

And we know that all things work together for good to them that love God.
To them who are the called according to his purpose. Romans 8:28

Her gaze lifted, inches from his face. The deep color of blue lured her closer. No man had ever made her feel what Bronson stirred inside.

He took her hand in his. "I'm sorry I didn't trust you after Corbin was killed. Instead, I pushed you away. I guess God's shown me there will always be challenging times in our lives. Even if we're grieving or sick, we can have each other. With God, nothing can stop us. But if you're still hesitant, I understand. Just know my feelings for you haven't changed since our talk at the hospital. I hope you can forgive me, and that we can try again."

She didn't need more time to think about her answer and leaned in, pressing her lips to his. His strong arms drew her body closer, and a good weakness surged clear through to her soul.

Her father always taught her that in our weakness, God is strong. Always there. Always answering our prayers.

Bronson pulled back, breathless. His hands cupped her jawline as he pressed his forehead against hers. "I don't want to live another minute without you."

"Neither do I."

He kissed the tears from her cheeks, his lips finding their way back to a deeper connection of forgiveness and longing. God had given her the desires of her heart and provided a purpose in her life—to be with Bronson Young, forever.

* * * * *

If you liked this story from Shannon Redmon, check out her previous Love Inspired Suspense books,

Cave of Secrets
Secrets Left Behind

Available now from Love Inspired Suspense! Find more great reads at www.LoveInspired.com.

Dear Reader,

Thank you for reading Bronson and Aggie's story. I've wanted to write about a female helicopter pilot for a long time and secretly wish I'd chosen that path as a young woman in my twenties, although it's probably much better that I write about them instead.

I want to thank my author friend, Jodie Bailey, and her husband, 1SG (R) Paul Bailey, for answering all my questions and helping me understand some of the details pertinent to this story. I hope I've portrayed these characters and the men and women of the United States Army in a strong, realistic way as the heroes they are. Thank you for risking and giving your lives, like my grandfather did, so we can live ours in peace.

As always, I love hearing from readers. Contact me through my website, shannonredmon.com, email me at shannon@shannonredmon.com or follow me on Goodreads, BookBub, and all other social media platforms.

Blessings and love,
Shannon Redmon

Get 4 FREE REWARDS!

We'll send you 2 FREE Books plus 2 FREE Mystery Gifts.

FREE Value Over **$20**

Both the **Harlequin® Special Edition** and **Harlequin® Heartwarming™** series feature compelling novels filled with stories of love and strength where the bonds of friendship, family and community unite.

YES! Please send me 2 FREE novels from the Harlequin Special Edition or Harlequin Heartwarming series and my 2 FREE gifts (gifts are worth about $10 retail). After receiving them, if I don't wish to receive any more books, I can return the shipping statement marked "cancel." If I don't cancel, I will receive 6 brand-new Harlequin Special Edition books every month and be billed just $5.49 each in the U.S. or $6.24 each in Canada, a savings of at least 12% off the cover price, or 4 brand-new Harlequin Heartwarming Larger-Print books every month and be billed just $6.24 each in the U.S. or $6.74 each in Canada, a savings of at least 19% off the cover price. It's quite a bargain! Shipping and handling is just 50¢ per book in the U.S. and $1.25 per book in Canada.* I understand that accepting the 2 free books and gifts places me under no obligation to buy anything. I can always return a shipment and cancel at any time by calling the number below. The free books and gifts are mine to keep no matter what I decide.

Choose one: ☐ **Harlequin Special Edition**
(235/335 HDN GRJV)

☐ **Harlequin Heartwarming**
Larger-Print
(161/361 HDN GRJV)

Name (please print)

Address   Apt. #

City   State/Province   Zip/Postal Code

Email: Please check this box ☐ if you would like to receive newsletters and promotional emails from Harlequin Enterprises ULC and its affiliates. You can unsubscribe anytime.

Mail to the **Harlequin Reader Service:**
IN U.S.A.: P.O. Box 1341, Buffalo, NY 14240-8531
IN CANADA: P.O. Box 603, Fort Erie, Ontario L2A 5X3

Want to try 2 free books from another series! Call 1-800-873-8635 or visit www.ReaderService.com.

HSEHW22R3

COUNTRY LEGACY COLLECTION

19 FREE BOOKS IN ALL!

Cowboys, adventure and romance await you in this new collection! Enjoy superb reading all year long with books by bestselling authors like Diana Palmer, Sasha Summers and Marie Ferrarella!